ESCAPE '56

ESCAPE '56

A Novel

RICHARD PANCHYK

TRIANGLE
SQUARE

books for young readers

an imprint of
Seven Stories Press
NEW YORK • OAKLAND • LONDON

For Mimi

✳ ✳ ✳

Seven Stories Press
www.sevenstories.com

Library of Congress Cataloging-in-Publication Data

Names: Panchyk, Richard, author.
Title: Escape '56 : a novel / Richard Panchyk.
Description: New York : Seven Stories Press/Triangle Square, 2023. |
   Audience: Ages 12 and up. | Audience: Grades 7-9.
Identifiers: LCCN 2022049122 | ISBN 9781644212530 (trade paperback) | ISBN
   9781644212547 (ebook)
Subjects: CYAC: Refugees--Fiction. | Emigration and immigration--Fiction. |
   Hungary--History--Revolution, 1956--Fiction. | Hungarians--United
   States--Fiction. | LCGFT: Biographical fiction. | Novels.
Classification: LCC PZ7.1.P357433 Es 2023 | DDC [Fic]--dc23
LC record available at https://lccn.loc.gov/2022049122

College professors and high school and middle school teachers may order free examination copies of Seven Stories Press titles. Visit https://www.sevenstories.com/pg/resources-academics or email academics@sevenstories.com.

Printed in the USA.

9 8 7 6 5 4 3 2 1

PRELUDE

Erzsi Molnár clenched her fists and tried to rest, but sleep wouldn't come. She lay there wondering what was going to happen next, the sound of gunfire in the distance jolting her awake. Her parents and older sister, Lili, had lived through World War II, when her city had been under Nazi control. From the limited things she'd heard, it was indeed an awful, frightening time. There were food shortages, and toward the end of the war, when the Allies—the Russians—were advancing on Budapest, there was bombing and shooting. Lots of bombing and shooting. Several of the city's buildings still bore the scars of those bullets. Now, it seemed that new scars were being made and she couldn't bear the thought. She wished she could go back in time. She wished she could have lived in the Golden Era.

Her parents had led an entirely different life before the Second World War. They were wealthy and successful. They were comfortable. Back then, Budapest was a cultural capital of central Europe, right alongside Vienna. And though Vienna still retained its worldly status, all that was long gone from Budapest. The family lived in what had been one of the fanciest buildings on the city's main boulevard, Andrássy Street. But it wasn't called that anymore. That was the old name. After the war it had been given the awful name Sztálin Street in honor of the leader of the Soviet Union. Yes, much had changed. Lifestyles, street names. And buildings—even this one was kind of run down now. On the surface, street names and building facades seemed to be a minor thing, but they were also a symbol of the so-called Iron Curtain that divided Hungary and other Eastern European countries from the rest of Europe and the world.

When the Nazis were vanquished back in 1945, the incoming Russians were seen as the saviors. For a minute anyway, as Mrs. Molnár liked to say. It soon became clear how they wanted to run things. In the name of "the people" they took away everything. They took away Mr. Molnár's coat store, the one his father, Erzsi's grandfather, had started many years ago. Even though Mr. Molnár still ran the store, he was not wealthy anymore. They even took possession of the family's apartment. When Mrs. Molnár and Lili went back to try to reclaim some of their furniture, they were mostly unsuccessful, but because the Russian soldiers thought the little blond girl was cute, they gave them back her baby furniture (she'd outgrown it all by now, but it still seemed like a victory) and gave Lili a thick chunk of bread with sugar sprinkled on top. Soviet generosity, such as it was. Sure, they still lived in the same building, but they now had to pay rent for a place they had once owned.

This was the only life Erzsi had ever known, yet she could see signs of old Budapest everywhere around her.

The elegant, gothic-style parliament buildings. The beautiful castle-like Halászbástya across the Danube River. The buildings along the former Andrássy Street, much like her own, were stately relics of a different era. The exuberant joy of this ancient city was still there, but it lately had the shadow of oppression hanging over it. She'd never known anything different, yet she could tell that this city had once been alive with an independent creative spirit.

***

Erzsi used to love looking out her apartment windows. They were big, broad old windows with two tall rectangular panes topped by a semicircular pane. Elegant from the outside and offering a great view, the windows faced the broad boulevard which, in another lifetime, had been filled with the bustling activity of people carrying bags of groceries and maybe even delicious pastries from the famous Gerbeaud Café, with its chocolate-dusted marzipan treats and decadent cakes.

This was the residential stretch of the street, so pedestrians were mainly shoppers coming back from stores, or men coming up from the nearby subway station after a day at work, or mothers pushing strollers as their babies pointed at birds chirping in the nearby trees. Erzsi used to watch the people walking and talking, and also look down at the sleek cars, taxis, and buses speeding along. She used to look across the street at the classical buildings built in a similar style to hers around the turn of the twentieth century. The ornate stonework, the elaborate balconies—her mother insisted that they were as fine as you'd see in any of the world's best cities, even Paris! This had always been home. Her home. Her street. She felt connected to it all.

But not now. Not anymore. Things had gone haywire. This did not feel like home. She did not want to go near the windows. The windows made her heart thud like crazy in her chest. In fact, her parents told her to stay away from the windows. The authorities had warned everyone to stay away from windows too. To stay in the hallways. But she didn't need to be told. The windows looked out onto a nightmare of epic proportions.

There were no shoppers to watch. There were no workers coming home from downtown. No strollers with happy cooing children.

No, now the street was deserted. Empty except for that monstrous machine. Empty except for the Soviet soldiers and their fearsome tank in the street, facing her building. Its gun was pointed at her parents' bedroom. In the city where she was born, in the building where she grew up, on her own street—she was now the enemy. She, her parents, her neighbors, her extended family and friends, they were all the enemies.

Erzsi had never seen a tank before. Not in person, only in war movies and in history books. Only in black and white. In real life the tanks were a dull, drab green, a color that made them seem even more menacing. These armored machines were clearly made to destroy anything in their way. It made for good action in films, but this was no film. This was real.

Though she was supposed to stay away from the window and the menacing barrel of the tank's big gun, she could not help but peek out to see the number painted on the side of the turret. They all seemed to have numbers. This one had a large "221" in white, and she imagined what it could mean. Perhaps there were at least 221 tanks in Budapest. Perhaps this tank had killed 221 people. Or destroyed 221 buildings. More likely it was just a representation of how impersonal all of this was to the Soviet government. The tanks were just numbers and so were the people of Budapest. Tank 221 was pointed at Building 743, perhaps. And more specifically at Person 12,087. Are we all just numbers to them? How many tanks and buildings and people were there in this city? It was too terrible to contemplate, yet doing so took her mind off worrying about the projectile that could come hurtling their way at any moment.

CHAPTER 1
August 1956

The Russian soldiers walked briskly through the park, their boot heels click-clacking on the pavement as they passed the bench where Erzsi sat contently. She barely even noticed them. Their presence around town was pretty common; it would be stranger not to see any soldiers on a given day. Her older sister, however, seemed to take more than a casual notice. Lili muttered under her breath, "Every time I see them, my throat closes up a little."

"Every time you see who?" Erzsi asked, even though she knew exactly what Lili meant. It was a lovely, late summer day, a day during which a ten-year-old girl (almost eleven!) would like to think of nothing except the warm sun and the gentle breeze.

Lili bit her lip and gestured with her head. "Them. The soldiers. Policing us like we are children."

"Umm, we *are* children." Sometimes when Lili talked, she said confusing things. But they were eight years apart, after all. It was to be expected. "And besides, they were just walking by. They didn't police anything."

Lili looked at her younger sister with a smirk. "Not us, you and me, here and now. I mean, us, all of us. Budapest. Hungary. All of us. Like we're children. And that is what policing means, walking by, watching over all of us. Always present."

"Hmm. Well, that's not right," Erzsi replied, even as her attention was grabbed by a young swan that had landed in the lake a few meters away. She pointed. "Ooh, look how pretty!" Városliget was a beautiful park only a few minutes' walk from their apartment. Its scenic lake was a delightful and relaxing place.

"You're too young to understand." Lili sighed, stood up, and stretched. "Come on. Time to go home. Mami is waiting for us."

"Can we just watch the swan for a few minutes?" She liked swans, especially after her mother mentioned that Grandpa had owned a business called Swan Linen Lending and its logo was a white swan silhouetted on a black background. The soldiers had stopped, apparently to admire the swan as well. One of them turned and tipped his cap at Lili. She looked at the ground, took Erzsi's hand, and said, "Come along, why don't we go home now?"

The taller of the soldiers said something in Russian to the other, laughed, and walked toward Lili. He was young, awkwardly red-cheeked, and dressed in what seemed to be a too-large drab army uniform, but his gun, shiny in its holster, was unnerving.

"Hey there, my dear," he said in halting Hungarian. "Lovely day, isn't it?"

"Yes, very." Lili kept her eyes fixed on the swan. Erzsi was excited for her sister. A soldier taking an interest in her? That was impressive. Too bad Lili seemed so bored.

"Is this your daughter? She's cute," the soldier said with a smirk and a wink. Daughter! That was a new one. But Lili was a mature eighteen and the soldier was trying to flirt.

"Yes, she is my daughter, and my husband is just over there. Géza!" she shouted to nobody in particular, adding in a broad wave for good measure. "Come here and meet this nice soldier!" It was a marked difference from other times in this very same park when Lili saw an attractive young man who was not in a Red Army uniform. In those cases, she'd send Erzsi over to say hello, wait ten seconds, and then come marching over with a stern warning to her young sister not to talk to strangers—then she and the stranger would strike up a conversation, which could potentially lead to a date. She had learned to exploit the benefits of having a little sister.

"Oh, I must get going now. Good day, madam." The soldier tipped his cap again and hurried after his comrade.

"Ha ha. Bravo. You should be in the movies," Erzsi told her sister, clapping softly.

"Yes. Wasted talent for sure. Now forget the stupid swan and let's go home!"

＊＊＊

"How was the park?" Mrs. Molnár asked when they got home.

"Fine," Lili said under her breath before going to her room and closing the door gently but fully.

"What's with her?" Mrs. Molnár asked Erzsi, who'd sat down at the kitchen table, waiting to see if her mother would bring her a glass of milk without being asked. And sure enough, Mrs. Molnár went to the cabinet, retrieved a short glass, and filled it up two-thirds with milk, then placed it on the table in front of her daughter. She was pleased to think she had her mother trained, at least in that regard.

"Thanks, Mami." She took a long and noisy gulp of milk.

"Oh, she's just moody because a solider flirted with her."

Mrs. Molnár shook her head slowly. "Flirted! That's disgusting."

"Well, he was kind of good-looking, to be honest." She laughed, but Mrs. Molnár was not having it.

"That's not funny, Erzsi. I don't like hearing these stories."

"It wasn't exactly a story. More like an observation." Erzsi knew she could get away with this kind of sauciness with her mother, but not with her father. He would not have wanted to hear it. But he was at work right now, making coats or selling them or maybe both. Coats for women and children. She never quite understood why he didn't make men's coats, but perhaps there was something fundamentally different about men's coats. Extra pockets? She made a mental note to ask him one day.

Mrs. Molnár shook her head and put her hands on her hips. She had long, elegant fingers and slender, smooth arms. Her face was pretty, a classic beauty still at the age of thirty-seven. Her chestnut-brown hair was always elegantly coiffed, and it reminded Erzsi of movie stars she'd seen on magazine covers at the newsstand. Great-Aunt Sara would whisper in Erzsi's ear every chance she got: "Your mother was quite the beauty when she was a few years older than you, sixteen or so. She should have been a model. Those hands holding a cigarette like this . . ." And Sara would attempt to demonstrate with her small, old, wrinkled hands.

"Erzsi!" Mrs. Molnár said. "I'm talking to you. Do I need to go ask her what happened? What did the soldier do? Did he touch her?"

"No! He didn't. And do not say a word, please. She will kill me if she knows I told you." And she would. Not physically but with guilt, dagger eyes, and hours-long silence. Bad enough.

Mrs. Molnár took the empty glass from Erzsi, rinsed it in the sink then left it there. She fiddled with some utensils in the drawer and then slammed it shut, which clattered loudly and made Erzsi sit up in her chair. "I don't like any of this. I wish it would stop. How long have we been stuck in this rut?"

"Rut?"

"You're too young," Mrs. Molnár said with a disappointed shake of her head.

"Too young for what?" She was constantly being told she was too old for this and too young for that. What was left for her to do? And just who was stuck in a rut here?

Mrs. Molnár sighed and sat down at the table. Her green eyes were bright in the afternoon light that was filtering in through the blinds. "Too young to know otherwise."

"Do you have to speak in riddles? I don't understand." Adults talk in riddles because they think we won't understand if they say the truth, Lili often said.

"Maybe it's better that way. Things were so different . . ." And Mrs. Molnár's voice trailed off and a faraway look appeared in her eyes. She stared straight through her daughter and into the past, a past where the sky was bluer and the trees greener and there were no soldiers and no bullet holes and Hungary was its own country. Her reverie was usually the same, and it was happening more often lately. For five or ten minutes, Erzsi would get to stroll with her through the past, the years long before she was born. Before the war. They would walk down the boulevard and Mrs. Molnár would describe how things used to be—the glory of the grand old Gerbeaud Café (only the most interesting people would eat there—artists and writers and mathematicians, though Erzsi could hardly imagine interesting mathematicians), the cheerful note in everyone's voices when they greeted one another, the street names that were infused with pride and history rather than communist terminology.

When these reveries ended, Erzsi usually said nothing and let her mother snap out of it gradually. But this time she said, "It sounds like you don't want to be here anymore."

This jolted Mrs. Molnár, who blinked at her daughter as if insulted. "Where on earth else would I want to be? Now go, go to your room. I have some cleaning to do before your father gets home, and there will be hell to pay if he finds me in here daydreaming!"

***

Erzsi went to her room grudgingly and read a little bit, but she popped her head out as soon as she heard the front door creak open about fifteen minutes later. Though Mr. Molnár was not always in a good mood when he returned from work, Erzsi was still always eager to see him, especially in the summer when school was out and she missed his presence more. If she sensed he was really in a foul mood, she'd retreat to her room and let him grouse and grumble for a few minutes first. This time, he seemed okay, by the sound of his greeting to his wife. So Erzsi skipped into the dining room with a smile and said, "Hi, Apu!"

Jancsi Molnár hung his hat and suit jacket on the coatrack and turned to face his daughter. "Hello, my little girl," he said in that gruff but affectionate manner of his. "How are you doing this afternoon?" His thinning jet-black hair was neatly slicked back as always, his face as clean-shaven as ever, expensive suit impeccably tailored to fit his slightly stocky frame. He presented a very clean, professional appearance and this made Erzsi proud. He was her father, out in the world making a good impression.

"Okay, I think," she said. Other than Lili's run-in with the soldier there was nothing much to report. She almost changed the topic, but she remembered to ask about his day first; a few weeks ago, she babbled on about herself for several minutes as soon as he came home, and he gently scolded her for being too self-centered. "And how was your day, Apu?"

"Oh, decent. We sold twelve coats. It was a pretty good day." Then his grin disappeared, and he turned to his wife, who was cutting potatoes. "Though it makes zero difference if I sell one or none or twelve or a hundred and thirty-seven. Because I am on salary at the company I founded. Because I'm not allowed to make a profit." He shook his head and looked up at the flaking paint way up on the high ceiling. Erzsi did not understand much about business, but she did know that before—before the war—her father worked for his own father at a large department store that sold coats, and the family was very wealthy. After the war, when the Soviets came in, you were not allowed to own your own business. The government owned everything and you worked for them.

"It's just not fair," Mrs. Molnár agreed with a particularly hard chop of her knife that sent a quarter of a potato across the counter, but she caught it before it became airborne and tossed it into the waiting pot. She knew that her husband was right, of course. But Mrs. Molnár was one to always make the best of things, so she was resigned to cheerily accept life as it was, more or less . . . except for things like soldiers making advances on her older daughter. She meant what she had just said, but she was not going to let that thought extend its bothersome tendrils throughout her mind and ruin her day. It was a lovely summer afternoon; the windows were open and birds were cheeping loudly just outside. Dinner would be on the stove soon enough, and afterward her sister was supposed to drop by and they would take a walk to the pastry café. But for now, she had to quell the raging tempest of her husband's anger about his business. He was still going on . . .

". . . and what's our motivation to do well if the profits are not distributed to us? This model is a failure except on paper, where it looks as if everyone will be fed and clothed and the state will watch us all. In reality, it's just a sham." He slammed his open hand on the dining room table a few times for effect. "A sham! I may as well be a street sweeper or a dogcatcher."

Erzsi quietly chuckled at the thought of her markedly nonathletic father trying to chase down energetic stray dogs on his short legs!

"Something funny, eh?" he asked with a scowl. Oops. It was more than a chuckle apparently. Lili liked to tell her sister: "You're either louder than you think, or quieter than you should be!" It was annoying to have a sister who was right about so many things.

"Sorry, no. Just I've always wanted a dog and at least then you could pick me a good one for free." She immediately regretted saying it when she saw the sour look still frozen on her father's face, but after a pause, his eyes lit up and his mouth twitched and he broke into a hearty peal of laughter. "Yes, that would work out perfectly. I'll give notice immediately at the coat shop. Or wait a minute, maybe I could transition by first making coats for dogs. To get myself prepared for all things canine."

They all laughed, the tension was broken, and soon the conversation shifted to other things. Erzsi helped her mother get the dinner ready, and Lili finally emerged from her bedroom to join the others for the meal.

CHAPTER 2
September 20

The warm August days melted by so quickly, days turned into weeks, and then suddenly it was time to go back to school. Summer was deeply mourned for the first few days, but after that Erzsi found herself fully immersed in the new school year—in her friends and the teachers and the familiar musty hallways of the old building. School books and messy notes and chewed-on pencils and confounding equations, it was all part of the new daily routine that she was starting to embrace once again.

Yet something was different this year. Even her friends noticed it. In the hallway that first week, bubbly blond Margit, Erzsi's best friend and sometimes worst enemy, recounted how her parents seemed so unhappy this summer on their annual vacation at Lake Balaton.

"They love that little cottage. But this time we had to cut our visit short because Pop said we were low on funds. Low on funds! He refused to say the word 'money.' He just kept saying 'funds.' Funds, funds. Low on them. They've dipped down. We stayed for five days instead of two weeks. Andor and I were so disappointed. My brother cried the whole way home, even though he's really too old to behave like that."

"But how much does it really cost to stay there? I mean, it's your grandma's old cottage, right? And your mom cooks the meals, same as at home."

"Yes, but it was more that . . . Pop needed to keep working. He could not afford to take the time off and lose another week's wages. He told us we could stay without him, but we took a vote and decided no, we wouldn't do that."

"Work work work! That's all my father talks about too. How he works his shirt off, and for what?" Erzsi could hear her father's voice complaining in her head. There was more to say but she stopped herself. Margit's father worked in the government, somewhere in the bowels of the bureaucracy, in some back office, an assistant to someone's assistant. But still. These days you had to be careful who you told what. At least that is what Lili told her on more than one occasion. "Wrong thing, wrong person, and we're all punished!" Lili had scolded her sister one day when Erzsi was recounting a conversation at a birthday party filled with adults who were not listening (or were they?) to the chatter of their kids.

But Margit seemed unaffected by Erzsi's words.

"My parents keep joking that I am almost old enough to get a job."

"By grace of God, we should not have to work," Erzsi shook her head. "Not until we are much older." Erzsi bristled at the suggestion. She wanted to just be a kid, not work! But things had changed. She thought of the stories Mami would tell her about the maids and cooks and nannies the family had many years ago. Now Mami did everything herself, as did most mothers in Budapest, no matter what their life had been like "before."

Margit put a finger to her lips. "Shhh!" she said. "You mustn't speak of religion here. Remember how Vivi got in trouble last semester when the teacher heard her praying before class?"

It was true, Margit was right. Talk of God and religion in Soviet-controlled schools was discouraged. There were plenty of churches holding regular services for millions of people, but officially, it was not something to be taught or discussed in school.

✳ ✳ ✳

That evening, while she was attempting to figure out some math problems, Erzsi overheard her parents talking about the United States for the third time in the last few days. Of course, as soon as she entered the room, they stopped talking, which only made it all the more mysterious. Why were they talking about America so much? And what was the secret? It was especially strange since her mother had never seemed particularly interested in the subject.

The United States was as foreign and exotic as Brazil, or Tibet, or the moon. It was a faraway place that she knew very little about. Little other than the fact that her uncle Ernő lived there. Uncle Ernő had left Hungary long before

Erzsi was born, before the war, even. He'd gone to America in 1939, and so Erzsi had never met or even spoken to him. She'd heard her father talk about him only here and there. Mr. Molnár sometimes called Ernő, but telephone calls were expensive and brief. He owned a bead-making business in New York, a big city that was far bigger than Budapest. It was like ten Budapests. It was hard for Erzsi to imagine how Uncle Ernő lived, or why he would have wanted to leave this place and his entire extended family. He was an American now, for sure. He'd even fought in the war, for the US army. She wondered if he remembered how to speak Hungarian properly. Maybe he talked like some American movie star now, like a cowboy or a gangster, and wore a fedora tilted at an angle to make him seem tough. One time, a couple of years back, he'd sent pink glass-bead necklaces to Erzsi and Lili as Christmas presents.

She forced herself out of her daydream and back to the present, to Budapest in September of 1956. She was ten years old now, almost eleven (very soon!). This was a great age to be. She had lots of friends, school was easy enough, and it was autumn, the season where the leaves along the boulevard were all turning red and yellow and orange. Not in America, here. Here in Budapest, where she and her family belonged, by the grace of God.

But something was different this fall. She could feel it. They did not own a television, but she heard the rumblings on the radio and from her parents. There was talk. The kind of talk that can lead to trouble. The people of Budapest were not happy under the thumb of the Soviet Union.

Mixed in with the usual crisp and fresh aura of autumn, the air was filled with restlessness and worry.

∗∗

Sometimes Erzsi wished she could snap her fingers and instantly be older—taller, smarter, more serious. She wanted to be an adult and to be able to have a say in the world, to be heard, and to change things. What things exactly, she was not sure. Whatever it took to make everyone feel happier. But when she mentioned this desire to her sister a few months ago, Lili shook her head quite firmly. "Don't wish for adulthood. It's young people who change things," she told Erzsi. Lili was eight years older and very wise, or so she liked to portray herself. She'd lived through the war (a subject about which she, like Mom and Dad, rarely spoke), and she'd known hard times. She was almost an adult, but at the same time still a kid.

"What do young people know about anything?" Erzsi asked her sister. "We're nothing, just children. You're eighteen but still dependent on our parents, like me."

"Ahh, but think of it, how often you've had a thought, a brilliant idea or inspiration about something in your life or the world, and Mom or Dad has brushed it off as childish. Think about when you get excited about something and go running up to Mami and you breathlessly tell her about your thoughts and she waves her hand and tells you to go play. They call it childishness, we call it imagination. We go to school and learn things about history, science, music, and art, and our heads are filled with ideas. Of course, we're bubbling with thoughts! The older people get, the more they forget how to be inspired, how to make history instead of repeat it."

"Maybe you're right." Erzsi clutched her doll, and in that moment felt a wave of repulsion come over her. A doll? Still? Wasn't it time to say good-bye to these childish things? Who makes history while clinging to a doll? She tossed the toy to her bed and rubbed her hands together fiercely.

"I know I'm right. And when change finally comes to Hungary, it will be the young people who make it happen." Lili got up from the edge of the bed and went to the mirror to brush her long blond hair, flaunting her best feature. She counted the strokes. Six . . . seven . . . eight . . . nine . . . ten. Erzsi thought of her own short, dark hair but quickly shoved the welling jealousy back into the deep recesses of her mind.

"When will it happen?"

Lili put the brush down and turned to face her sister. "Oh, it could be any day now, to be honest. There are rumblings among my friends."

"Rumblings? Like an angry stomach?" She laughed.

"Yes. Talk. Hushed talk, not-so-hushed talk. About protests that need to happen. Making our voices heard. Demanding change." Lili checked the mirror one last time and nodded in approval.

"It will be a good change, right?" Erzsi asked.

"Well, change can be hard, but sometimes change is needed. It can't get much worse than this, right? So yeah. A good change."

Erzsi was not sure her sister was right about that. Things could always be worse than they were. Maybe that was a childish thing to think, but then again, Erzsi was still young. She grabbed her doll and told her mother she was going outside to play. She would leave the hair brushing and the political rumblings to her sister for now.

CHAPTER 3
October 4

From the hallway, Erzsi could hear the distant yet distinct strains of an accordion. She shook her head and sighed. Ivan was on his way over, again. Lili's boyfriend was nice enough, but he was sure fixated on that accordion. Sometimes he would serenade Lili from his balcony across the courtyard. The echo effect only amplified the sound. And on those evenings when he came calling, he brought the contraption with him, strapped around his neck. It was not exactly clear whether Lili loved or hated it, but she made a good show of playing along and clapping when he finished a tune.

Sure enough, a minute later, there was a knock at the front door. Lili bounded out of the bedroom, nearly knocking her sister over in the process, calling out a half-hearted apology as she passed. Lili flung open the door and there was Ivan, a stocky, barrel-chested young man, his short brown hair neatly parted in the center and combed back, a broad smile plastered on his square face. He kissed her cheeks and they exchanged pleasantries, then he followed her into the living room, where Mrs. Molnár was sitting reading a book.

"Greetings, Mother!" he said, bowing his head in a manner he knew amused her. She smiled and returned the greeting. Though she knew that the pleasant silence in the apartment was about to be broken, she kept reading for a few more seconds, right up until the first jarring note emerged from Ivan's shiny red accordion. Mrs. Molnár then quickly slipped the tattered paper bookmark into place and put the book on her lap.

It was not a song, however, it was just Ivan warming up the instrument, though he'd already been playing it most of the way to their place. After a few bars of random music, he seemed satisfied and began to chat.

Lili sat down on the divan next to her sister. Erzsi could have retreated to her room but she decided to stay, mainly so she wouldn't feel left out, but also for the chance to make a few wry comments about the forthcoming concert and tease her sister. And it did seem like a concert was imminent, since Ivan remained standing with his accordion as the mother and her daughters sat waiting for the show to begin. But Ivan, having duly warmed his instrument, now was warming himself up, calming his own nerves, telling a few jokes, and complimenting Lili on her outfit.

"The weather has been outstanding so far this October, hasn't it?" Ivan asked. "The leaves in their colors. Autumn is beautiful!"

"Yes, it is. Both here and in America, from what I understand," Lili said looking at her mother. Now and then she'd do this, subtly trying to pressure her parents into considering moving. Ivan and Erzsi laughed at Lili's reply, but

Mrs. Molnár managed only a wan smile. The mentions of America seemed to be increasing lately.

"And now, are you ready for some music?" Ivan asked. He began to play without waiting for a reply. At least he was not singing too. There was something to be thankful for! As usual, Ivan mixed known songs with made-up ones he created based on the small talk that had just happened. First, he played the old folk tune "Nékem Olyan Asszony Kell" ("I Need a Woman"), which perked Mrs. Molnár up, since she often sang that song while doing chores around the house. And indeed, though she listened silently at first, when Ivan played it a second time, she began to sing along: "I need a woman, even if she's sick, who'll get up, and cook dinner. She waits, waits, waits, waits, for her husband to come home." Eww, thought Erzsi, why would anyone sit around waiting for a husband to come home?

Ivan beamed at his success, proud at how quickly his hands and fingers moved to make the accordion do his bidding. Mrs. Molnár sang and Lili clapped along. Erzsi just rolled her eyes and wondered if her own future boyfriend would be as annoyingly adorable (or was it adorably annoying?) as this. She hoped not. She wanted a boyfriend who was serious, studious, and quiet, and who would not need to be in the spotlight all the time. Ivan played all the verses of the folk song one more time, and Lili joined in the singing.

Now that the mood was lighter, Ivan decided to make up a song. As he paused between tunes, he noted the smirk on Erzsi's face and gave her a wink. Erzsi averted her eyes. Annoying! Yet adorable. He noodled a bit on the accordion until he found a tune. And as punishment for feeling thankful that Ivan was not going to sing, that is exactly what he began to do—he started to sing along to his invented tune, which had the sound of a lilting polka.

"America, it waits for you, but if you go, I'll be so blue (so blue). Stay with me I'll play more songs. I can't be away from you for long (so long). The leaves are pretty but so are they here, the sun is bright, the skies are clear (so clear). America will have to wait, for Hungary is your only fate (your fate)!"

Mrs. Molnár applauded sharply at the end of the song, which meant she approved of its message, but also that it was now time for her to start preparing dinner. Her husband would be home soon. "She waits, waits, waits, waits, for her husband to come home," Mrs. Molnár sang as she made her way into the kitchen.

Ivan put the accordion down in the corner, but the loud and festive music lingered in the air. He knew he had about a half an hour before Lili's father came home from work. The two sat down on the sofa.

"Promise me you won't leave me for another country!" Ivan said, taking her hands in his.

"Promises are for fools," she said.

"Exactly. Look at me—if ever there was a fool, here I am!"

Erzsi's disgust at their banter quickly melted away when Ivan asked her if he could play a song just for her, any song she liked. His eyes twinkled and for a moment she got caught up in his charm. She clapped her hands and said, "Az a Szép!"

This was not the first time she'd asked him to play the short, popular folk song. He nodded and smiled, placed his fingers and started to play, as he and Lili sang together, "They are beautiful, they are beautiful, those whose eyes are blue, whose eyes are blue. Though mine are, though mine are dark blue. I'm not beautiful enough to my sweetheart true. Beautiful are those whose eyes are blue, whose eyes are dark black." The song was best performed on violin, but Ivan did it justice with his instrument. Erzsi applauded as her sister and Ivan laughed. As the three of them chatted happily, blue-eyed American girls danced in Erzsi's head.

CHAPTER 4
October 6

One of the things Erzsi loved most about her city was the cuisine. Budapest was a city of delicious food. Hungarian cuisine was known worldwide for its savory stews, beef *gulyás*—or "goo-losh," as Erzsi heard an American visitor pronounce it once—being the most famous. Aside from the meals that Mrs. Molnár cooked on a daily basis, dishes such as *paprikás csirke* (a simple chicken dish that was a Hungarian classic) and *rakott krumpli* (sliced potatoes, hard-boiled eggs, and ham, layered with sour cream . . . just thinking about it made Erzsi's mouth water!), there were plenty of other treats to be had all around the city. In the old days, before the war, they had a cook who prepared lunch and dinner on days when the family didn't go out to eat at Gundel's or one of the other popular restaurants. In fact, Grandfather, who had died long before Erzsi was born, counted Gundel's and other restaurants among his clients—his linen-cleaning business specialized in tablecloths and napkins. The family had enjoyed many a discounted meal thanks to Grandfather's connections. A large photograph taken in 1935 hung in the Molnárs' bedroom, of the lavish wedding banquet of Mrs. Molnár's sister at the fancy Gellért Hotel. Tall glasses were filled with beer and the plates on the table were full of mouth-watering food.

But times had changed. There were no more discounts to be had, no more lavish banquets. The Soviets had taken over the family's linen business, along with everyone else's businesses. The family cook was long gone now, and dining out was too expensive to do more than a few times a month. Sweetshop treats were cheaper, thank good-ness, and were enjoyed occasionally. Popular cafés such as Gerbeaud and Ruszwurm served a delectable array of pastries and hot drinks to wash them down. The *krumpli mignon* was a favorite of Erzsi's. A pastry made to look like a potato, it was really a round plain cake filled with choc-olate cream and then covered with marzipan and dusted with the finest cocoa powder.

There were sweet treats to be made at home too, such as *palacsinta*, or crepes, which were made with a simple egg, flour, and milk batter that was poured into a hot, oiled pan and fried. These thin pancakes could be filled with jam or cocoa or sugar and rolled up. Oh, how she loved them! During the last few weeks, her mother started to teach Erzsi how to make them. There was no recipe—it was all done by feel. The batter had to be just so thick when you poured it so it would congeal properly in the pan and cook without sticking. "Watch and learn," Mami told her daughter. "It's the only way." She'd crack several eggs, and then add flour little by little, mixing the two ingredients together. When the mixture reached a certain thickness and the dough clung to the fork just so, then Mami added the milk, again, little by little and stirring all the while. Erzsi wondered whether there was an easier way, but her mother reminded her that some things in life you just had to feel your way through—that depending on the size of the eggs and humidity of the day, you might need more or less flour and therefore more or less milk.

Lili knew how to make *palacsinta*, as well as some other dishes, and once in a rare while she would have free rein of the stove. But typically, Mrs. Molnár preferred to retain control over her kitchen. Erzsi suspected it would be a year or two before she was allowed to attempt *palacsinta* on her own, but that was okay. There was no rush to grow up too fast. For now, she was content to enjoy the food her mother cooked and absorb any lessons that she was offered.

Though Erzsi could not enjoy her city's food in the same luxurious, carefree way her parents had growing up in the pre-communist, pre-war era, she loved every mouthful of the food she ate, no matter who had prepared it. Hungarian food was a huge part of her daily happiness, and she could not imagine life any other way.

CHAPTER 5
October 13

In Erzsi's young eyes, Nadia Andor was an exotic creature. By the age of eighteen, she had already established herself as a fencing champion, and now at the age of twenty, Nadia had made the Hungarian Olympic team and would soon be getting on an airplane heading to Melbourne, Australia, for the 1956 Summer Olympics.

Erzsi could not take her eyes off this beautiful, mature, and talented young woman who also happened to be her cousin. Nadia's dark, wavy hair, perfect silky-smooth skin, penetrating brown eyes, and girlish features were hypnotic on their own, but picturing this young woman with a sword in hand, slashing and dodging and lunging, was breathtaking. As Nadia and her mother sipped hot cocoa and coffee with the Molnárs at the dining room table, their banter bubbled with excitement over her impending departure.

"So, Summer Olympics?" Lili said. "What's with the delay, summer's over and the games don't start till November!"

Nadia smiled, long fingers wrapped around her coffee cup. "Well, maybe so here, but summer in the Southern Hemisphere is during our winter."

"Nadia has studied every possible fact about Australia, so she's going to be well prepared," her mother, Regina, interjected proudly, patting her daughter's back. "While all the other athletes struggle to get acclimated, my girl will be able to focus solely on her sport." When one accounted for their age difference, Nadia and her mother looked quite similar, but the daughter had a warm, joyful glow that her nervous mother could never manage.

"I wouldn't say every possible fact. I know a little about kangaroos and couple of facts on koalas and the climate. That's about it!" She laughed her soft girlish laugh, one that would fool any competitor into thinking she would be easy prey. But in fact, Nadia was quite fierce with a foil or an épée. They'd seen her in a competition four years ago and even at age sixteen she was a dynamo, performing what seemed as much like a gymnastics exhibition as a fencing performance.

"Well, I hope you crush your opponents, injure them, disable them, or whatever you're supposed to do!" Erzsi said, eyes wide. *And come home with a gold medal*, she might have added if she wasn't afraid of jinxing it.

Erzsi's father chuckled at this outburst, but Nadia smiled slightly and took her cousin's hand in her own. She looked right into Erzsi's eyes. "Oh, but fencing is not about vanquishing or injuring. Not like you see in the movies. Not like in *The Mark of Zorro*. It's actually very calculated. Mathematical almost. It's all about points. Every touch is a point for you. It's about outsmarting your opponent, anticipating, counteracting, defending. And in so doing, much elegance and footwork is required. It's more like choreography than vanquishing an enemy."

Jancsi Molnár made a lunging motion with one hand and almost knocked over his coffee. "Looks to me like vanquishing!" he said, trying to divert attention from his near mishap.

"Yes, and you were about to vanquish your coffee all over the tablecloth," said his wife with a raised eyebrow. Everyone laughed briefly, and then they were all silent for a few seconds, except for a few sips and the scraping of forks against plates in concerted efforts to round up the last of the delicious fudge icing that topped the chocolate layer cake from Gerbeaud. They were keenly aware that Nadia was about to leave Hungary, something many would love to do, even if only temporarily. She would see another part of the world. Firsthand!

"Teach me how to fence, cousin!" Erzsi said, standing so abruptly that her chair clattered backward to the floor, generating a loud *tsk tsk!* from her mother. Not that Erzsi was terribly interested in the sport itself, but the idea of telling all her classmates that she learned how to fence from an Olympic athlete, that was quite exciting!

"Erzsi, this is not the place," her mother interjected, sitting up straight and clasping her hands together on the table. "Maybe another time."

"No, it's okay. If my little cousin wants to learn, I can probably show her a few things." Nadia took the cloth napkin from her lap, dabbed the corners of her mouth, and stood up. Her kind eyes scanned the room. Then she pointed. "Over there, Uncle, may we use those umbrellas?"

"Go ahead!" Jancsi was amused. His family was a source of endless entertainment, and entertainment was always welcomed—provided it occurred at the right time. He was well aware that on another day the suggestion of a fencing tutorial in his apartment might have set him off. But the coffee and the cake left him feeling very amenable.

Erzsi sprang up and flew to the umbrella stand before Nadia could budge. She applauded her young cousin. "Well now, with reflexes and speed like that, you should be a fencing champion in no time!"

The girls moved into the living room while the audience at the dining room table turned their chairs so they could see this spectacle unfold. Mrs. Molnár poured more coffee while Nadia went through a few basics (which by now were so instinctual that she had to think in order to put them in words): the proper stance, the balance, the position of the arms, how to hold the "sword." Erzsi tried her best to emulate this artful cousin of hers. Next were a few drills on how to lunge, and Nadia seemed satisfied.

"These may look harmless," she said holding up an umbrella. "But they're probably more dangerous than the actual foils I use, since when I fence, I am in a protective suit and the foil is highly flexible. So, we're going to take it slowly and try not to destroy my uncle's living room."

Mr. Molnár laughed, "That's a good point. If you were to destroy the living room, I'd want a film crew here to capture it, so they can use it in the new Hungarian version of *Robin Hood.*"

"Wait, wait," said Mrs. Molnár. She went to the kitchen and brought back a couple of small dinner rolls. She stuck one on the tip of each umbrella and Nadia applauded. "Very smart, Auntie, now we can assure that only bread crumbs and not blood will be spilled today."

The girls took up their positions, and Nadia was proud of how Erzsi held her umbrella in just the right position, though her feet were a little off the mark. But this was not the time to nitpick, or her cousin would lose interest. "All right, on three, we begin. Remember, attack and defense often happen virtually in the same moment. One, two, three!"

Nadia began with a fake-out step to the right, then moved left and forward, though slowly, far slower than she would in a match. Erzsi anticipated and moved to her left, then lunged with the umbrella, which was met by Nadia's umbrella. They tangled briefly before Nadia disengaged and sidestepped, then lunged and touched her cousin's arm with the roll. The adults clapped and Erzsi shrugged. "Best of three," she said. Nadia nodded, and they retreated to their places for the countdown. Though Erzsi made several lunges, Nadia was able to avoid them all quite deftly. The more Erzsi tried, the more desperate and undisciplined her attempts became. And then Nadia struck, tapping the inside of her cousin's thigh. The shock of the surprise attack made Erzsi lose her grip on the umbrella, which landed a few inches from a ceramic vase on the coffee table. "Oof!" she yelped, and quickly retrieved her weapon. "What did I do wrong, cousin? I tried so hard."

"Exactly. You tried too hard. You abandoned the method and just jabbed at me with reckless abandon. In doing so you compromised your ability to defend. You were unorganized and unbalanced, and I saw openings. Sometimes the best offense is defense. When you successfully dodge me, you throw me off balance for a split second, and that can be enough to score a point."

"All right, all right, Nadia, that's enough," her mother said, waving her empty coffee cup in the air. "She wanted a quick lesson not a seminar."

"This is the quick lesson. Be glad you don't have to train like I do, five days a week for hours at a time!" Nadia plucked the rolls from the umbrella tips and handed them back to her aunt, who promptly placed them in front of her husband. "Here. Dinner is served," she said, laughing. He quickly took a bite from one, to everyone's mock disgust.

"Not every day one gets to eat the tip of an Olympian's sword!" he said, chewing thoughtfully.

"Okay then, it's time for us to be getting home," Regina Andor said, glancing at her watch. She was sociable to a point, but when she was done, that was it. In that way she was like her brother.

"I can't believe when I see you again, you'll have been in the Olympics," said Erzsi.

"That is, if I decide to come back to Hungary. Maybe I'll stay in Australia with the kangaroos and koalas and the winter that's summer!" Nadia was tickled by her own words. Nobody was officially allowed to just leave Hungary, not these days, not without considerable trouble.

Politics! She was pretty sure it would be the first time anyone on her fencing team would be leaving Hungary. And if she were lucky, she might get to compete in the 1960 Olympics—in Rome no less! She looked around her uncle's apartment and realized none of her family might ever get to leave the country. She hugged her little cousin extra tightly as she said good-bye. "I will see you in December, with lots of stories to tell! And if not, I'll send a postcard!" She winked and then walked out the door.

CHAPTER 6
October 15

János Molnár sat in his stuffy office, in the back corner of the shop on Király Street. His faded ledger book was open to the month of September. The blue ink of his pen had filled line after line of gross receipts and salary payouts for his employees, both salesclerks and coat makers. Well, calling them his employees, that was a bit of a misnomer. Sure, they did work for him, but this was not his store. It belonged to the state. To the People of Hungary, more (or less) accurately. He studied the September numbers. There was a profit, a positive balance at the bottom of the last column. But that money was not going into his pocket. That money would not be going toward a new dress for his wife or new toys for Erzsi. No, the extra money was not his to take. He received a salary just like the others.

He leaned over and sniffed the ledger book. Its yellowed pages had a sweet and musty scent. This grand old record book had been his father's before him, back when the shop belonged to Papa, before the craziness of the war—and before Papa's death in '43. It was a complete record of the financial side of the business over the last twenty years.

János flipped back the pages to 1938, the heyday of the store, and looked at his father's scrawlings. Back then they advertised in all the major newspapers and magazines, and they issued catalogs to their customers, sixteen-page illustrated brochures featuring all the latest styles of woman's and children's coats and outerwear. Customers bought coats that came on embossed hangers with the store name and address, stuffed neatly into handled paper bags proudly displaying the store name. Ahh, 1938 had been a very good year, like the ones before it. That string of profitable years had helped his parents buy the summer cottage on Svábhegy, the hill across the Danube River. Another possession that was no longer his.

Just be thankful you are employed, he told himself. You can feed your family; you have a place to live. You are alive—during the war, this was definitely not a guarantee. So, all things considered, was it so terrible that he no longer owned the family business? He thought of his younger daughter. Her whole life had taken place in this stifling environment. But maybe that was okay. Not knowing anything else makes living this way easier. The censorship, the state-run newspapers, the government ownership of businesses—this was all she knew. That thought comforted him for a second, but he quickly reconsidered. It doesn't matter if you are born in a cage and that's all you know, sooner or later, you will get sick of the cage and realize there must be more.

He remembered when he was a boy Erzsi's age, visiting his father here in the store, walking past the racks of coats along the main aisle and coming into this very office to see Papa in this chair with this very ledger book opened on this desk. Papa twirling his mustache the way he used to when he was lost in thought. Jancsi smiled at the memory. Everyone in the store knew him back then, most of them were longtime employees who had seen him as a baby in a stroller, pushed to the store by his mother. Many of the salesclerks had watched him grow up over the years . . .

"Hey Jancsi!" they'd call out. "How are you?"

They treated him like the store owner's kid. They knew they had to be nice to him, so they were. Was that the only reason? Maybe. He was a bit of a brat back then. Every time he walked the aisle lined with coatracks, he ran his hands along the coats, making sure he touched every one, sometimes even yanking one off the rack and letting it drop to the floor. He did it because he could. Because nobody would dare stop him. He did it because if any other kid came in the store and did that, they'd be reprimanded and escorted out. Even at such a young age he had known that this would all be his one day. His younger brother, Ernő, had expressed zero interest in coats, and so it was a foregone conclusion that the store would go to Jancsi.

"This will all be yours one day!" Papa liked to remind him with a sweeping gesture of his short arms. And now it was, only it wasn't. He closed the ledger book and slipped it back into the desk drawer, turned the little brass key to lock it, and put the key ring back in his pocket.

"Mine," he thought. Hungary had been through so much change since those days. The aftermath of the war had changed things drastically. Though the Soviets themselves were not running things, the Hungarian Communist Party installed leaders with the full approval and permission of the Soviet Union. They were but puppets at the hands of the Russians, and life was subject to the whims of the Hungarian leaders and their Soviet counterparts—first Stalin and now Khrushchev. Hungarian post-war politics was hard to keep up with. Even in the last few years alone, much had happened. The unpleasant leadership of Prime Minister Mátyás Rákosi meant five years of brutal policies—arrests, relocations, and deportations of thousands of people, including thousands within the Community Party. There was the arrest of Cardinal Mindszenty for "treason" (because he openly opposed communism) and his sentence of life in prison—a leader of the Catholic Church no less! Thankfully, a few years ago, Rákosi had been replaced as prime minister by Imre Nagy, a more sympathetic leader, but last year Rákosi had Nagy removed from power before he himself was recalled by the Soviet Union and replaced with the current leader, an equally unpleasant politician named Ernő Gerő. They were all Communists who served at the whims of the Soviets, but Nagy had been the least hostile of them.

Jancsi leaned back as far as the chair would let him and put his feet up on the desk. There had been times when he thought he was in danger of being arrested. As a somewhat prominent businessman, he worried that he'd be deemed a threat, for some reason or another. It did not take much for the secret police to act. Last year, a woman came into the store ranting about how she was overcharged for one of his coats, threatening to spread the word about this "injustice" that was an affront to "our socialist existence." He was almost certain she was harmless, but he knew that a "tip" to the secret police about his unfair business practices could be enough to get him sent away.

If only the store were really his. He sighed. Even if, for argument's sake, the store had still been his right now, the profits were only a tenth of what they used to be. The people of Budapest simply did not have that kind of money to spend anymore. The fancier, more expensive, and more fashionable coats had been discontinued in favor of cheaper, more basic ones. There was only one remnant of the past, a single tan wool car coat with a lush brown fur collar and a soft fur lining. It was the last of its kind they'd made. How many years ago was that now? Seven? More? He'd thought about keeping it on the showroom floor, but the risk of it being stolen was too great these days when many were poor and a quick theft and resale of something like this could feed a family for a couple of weeks. So instead, it hung in his personal closet in the office, waiting for someone to ask, "Do you have anything more expensive, maybe a fur-lined coat?" But in the last three years nobody had even inquired. He walked to the closet and opened the door. The coat was attractive, for sure. It would be good to have the money from this sale, he thought as he ran his hand over the mink collar, before reminding himself that selling it would give him no extra profits. Nobody would even know if the coat just ceased to exist. And come to think of it, Anna could use a new coat.

In that moment, he decided. He abruptly took the coat off its hanger, sending dust flying and making him cough. He put it into a garment bag and flung the heavy bundle over his shoulder. He'd earned it with his sweat over the years! It was too old by now anyway; nobody wants a seven-year-old coat. Surely a write-off, he told himself. Satisfied with his excuse for taking the coat, he grabbed his briefcase, locked the office door, and left the store. To heck with the government and their rules. "This is my store!" he said loudly as he slammed the shop door behind him.

CHAPTER 7
October 16

Ever since she was small, Erzsi was obsessed with the mysterious woman in the large, dark painting with the thick and ornate golden frame. It hung over the sofa on the wall of the living room, an overpowering presence in an apartment of attractive things, almost all of which dated to before the war. And overpowering was not an exaggeration—even now that she was almost eleven years old, the painting was still taller than she was.

When she was smaller, Erzsi would come into the room just to sit and stare at the painting. In particular, at the woman in the painting. She was a young woman with short, slightly curly dark hair, and she was seated, with a paintbrush in hand. An artist! She wore what looked like a beautiful white satin dress, but on closer inspection it was some kind of painter's smock or apron. She sat in profile, facing a canvas on an easel. But the canvas was at a tilt, facing away from Erzsi. The woman's expression was a little lost in the smoke and grime of the decades, but she did not seem happy. She seemed melancholy at best. Perhaps contemplative. Oh, the questions Erzsi used to ask her mother!

"Where did the painting come from?"

"My father bought it. He loved art, or more precisely, he loved to acquire art. So he bought this."

"How much did he pay?"

"I have no idea, Erzsi. It was long ago, when I was just a child myself. And anyway, your grandfather never spoke of such things. Now and then he'd come home with a new painting wrapped in brown paper, tucked under his arm. He'd unwrap it and hang it, and that was that. We didn't ask questions."

"Who is the woman?"

"I don't know, Erzsi. She's just a woman. Maybe she existed or maybe she was just a figment of the painter's imagination."

This thought was abhorrent to Erzsi. How could a painter conjure up a person entirely from imagination? No, this woman had to be real. The painter had visited her studio and painted her as she sat before the canvas. But when Erzsi mentioned this scenario to her mother, she was met with the kind of laughter reserved for the fanciful notions of children.

"Oh no, no, no. Chances are, if this woman was real, she was specifically posed like this. Artists use models and they pose them in whatever position or scene they want to paint."

"So, he picked a woman and made her dress like this and sit here in a studio holding a brush for hours?"

"No! The model can sit in a cheap wood chair in an empty apartment, or in the artist's studio, or wherever.

The artist only needs the model's body, her face, her pose. The rest of the scene can be painted later, from a photograph or from something else. He could have her sit in a dark studio and then paint her sitting in a field of daisies."

That her mother knew so much about art was astonishing and also unnerving. Erzsi had a suspicion that the woman in the painting was really her grandmother. Grandma had died a few years before, and of course by then she looked nothing like the model. But in the old framed photo of Grandma on Mami's dresser, she saw a striking resemblance. Had Grandpa paid the artist to paint his wife? Could it be? She dared not ask, because she did not want to be ridiculed.

The older Erzsi grew, the more questions she had about the painting, and the less comfortable she felt asking them. These were questions that she bandied about in her head—or even out loud if nobody else was at home at the time. "Why are you so sad, Marta?" she asked the woman. She had to give her a name; it seemed only right. The older Erzsi grew, the more off the whole scene felt. The woman was painting something, but the viewer was not allowed to know what. Why? It would be far more interesting to see what was being painted . . . and yet the mystery was intriguing. But actually, was Marta even painting at all? Was she just sitting there thinking about painting? Why was she holding the palette so it was facing the viewer? Wouldn't it be facing her, the painter? Erzsi tried to study Marta's face. One afternoon she even went so far as to stand on the sofa (forbidden!) and get a closer look, but she lost her footing and fell over backward, onto the sofa and then the floor. She cursed Marta. It was the first time she'd cursed out loud, and that made her laugh. She stayed there, sprawled out on the floor, looked up at the painting, and said, "Marta, you should finish your stupid painting already. It's been years and you must be tired of sitting there, just like I'm tired of looking at nothing. Show me the painting already!"

Once in a while, Erzsi would get a pencil and paper and sketch what she imagined Marta to be painting. A man with a straw hat, a field with red poppies, or maybe it was a still life of fruit and candles. A few months ago, when she was about to do another imagined painting, it struck her. Marta had nothing in front of her. There was no bowl of fruit, no model posing, no scenery. She was painting without a subject. This made the artwork even more beguiling and mysterious. It was a painting of a painter who was painting nothing. That made Erzsi sad, and lately she'd taken to pretending that she was Marta's model. She'd strike a pose in the living room, imagining the woman had given her instructions, picturing the studious glances and the brushstrokes that followed. "Will you let me see it when you're done?" she'd ask the painting, looking carefully until she swore she saw Marta nod.

The most recent investigation Erzsi thought to perform was to read the signature at the bottom right of the painting. Szüle. Not a common name. If she could locate this painter, and chances were he lived in Budapest, she could ask him herself! She grabbed the telephone directory and leafed through its thin pages so hastily she ripped one in half. When she finally got to "Sz" she sighed. There were no "Szüle" listings at all. Maybe he lived elsewhere in Hungary. He must! It would require further research, in the library there was probably a directory for all of Hungary, and he would be in there. Or she? Maybe Szüle was the woman in the painting, maybe it was a self-portrait, an intriguing possibility.

She practiced her introduction out loud, several times: "Hello, Mr. Szüle? My name is Erzsi Molnár and we have one of your paintings in our house. It's the big giant one with the woman sitting there with a paintbrush and a palette and I have some questions for you, please don't hang up!" She even had a speech planned in case someone else picked up the phone: "He's not there at the moment? Well, if he could call me back, my number is 311-643 and I am really anxious to talk to him!"

Her heart sank when she finally made it to the library and found the painter in a thick encyclopedia called *Hungarian Artists 1600–Present*. His name was Péter Szüle and he had died in 1944. Long gone. Now the painting was even more intriguing to her. And also, she wanted to know why her grandfather had purchased this to begin with, assuming that Marta was not Grandma—why would anyone want a giant painting of a random woman in their house? She asked that singular question to Lili one day and her sister shrugged. "It's art. Every painting is random. Every lake, cottage, bowl of fruit, herd of cows, woman posing—they're all just random things and places. Artists can't have a personal connection to everything they paint, that would be too limiting. Look at the other paintings here. They all fall into that category. This one is just bigger than the others, is all."

Maybe Lili was right. What point was there in obsessing over this one when there were ten others on the various walls? Because this one was so big, and so odd. That's why. Yes, there was a small painting of a man with a beard in the other room. But she never gave that one any thought.

CHAPTER 8
October 18

The incessant questions and comments about the Szüle painting this summer and autumn were met with patience that eventually turned to bored exasperation. Mrs. Molnár chided herself for not encouraging her younger daughter's inquisitive nature, but what could she do? She didn't have the answers.

And then she had an idea.

Kálmán.

Miklós Kálmán was a painter who had done a couple of portraits of her sister years ago. He was a family friend, of sorts. They'd known him for fifteen, maybe twenty years now. She would ring him up and explain the situation and ask whether her daughter could go over there and spend an afternoon at his apartment, which also served as his studio. The old guy was a bit eccentric but seemed trustworthy enough for an unaccompanied visit. Not surprisingly, Kálmán was perfectly willing to entertain Erzsi, so long as she brought grapes. He loved grapes and made sure to specify the type and quantity—light-red grapes from the Tokaj region, two big handfuls worth. Erzsi could stop by the next day after school. Mrs. Molnár clapped her hands at the thought that her inquisitive daughter's mind might be put at ease by some answers from this established artist.

"Just be sure to refuse if he offers to paint you," she warned as she put the grapes into a paper bag and handed them to Erzsi.

"And why would I refuse that?" Erzsi asked. The chance to be someone's Marta? She would make sure to smile so as not to look so depressed like the woman on their living room wall. Though maybe holding a smile for so long was impossible, hence Marta's expressionless expression.

"When your aunt sat for him, she wound up spending eight hours there, and he only paid her twenty forint. So, no paintings. A quick sketch, maybe." Mrs. Molnár winked at her daughter.

School was impossibly long the next day; Erzsi could not stop thinking about the visit and the thought that had just struck her that morning—maybe Kálmán knew Szüle! And then her questions could really be answered!

The moment the teacher let the class go, she flew down the hallway, almost knocking over her friend Margit, and rushed out the door. It was a twenty-minute walk to the painter's home, but she made it into a ten-minute sprint. Breathless, she bounded up the stairs to the second floor of his building and double-checked the slip of paper with his apartment number—2D. Yes, this was it. She knocked rather meekly, waited, then knocked again so hard that her knuckles hurt. The forest-green door swung open, and a short bald man greeted her by grabbing the bag of grapes from her and nodding, his bulging bright blue eyes full of excitement.

"Come, come," he said, gesturing as he turned to go back inside the apartment. The air smelled of stale cigarettes and oil paint. They were standing in his bedroom. On the right was his bed, a messy jumble of blue and white striped blankets and sheets. On the left, a high dresser littered with glass vases filled with dried (dead?) flowers. On the walls all around were paintings, lots and lots of paintings, most of them slightly crooked. Erzsi did not have the chance to look at any of them closely, because the painter kept walking on ahead and then to the right through a broad doorless entryway into another, much bigger room. This room was like a museum—three huge, beautifully executed religious paintings (even larger than the Szüle) adorned each of the walls in equally stunning gold frames, surrounded by smaller ones of all types—landscapes, portraits, still lifes—also in elegant frames. At the center of the room was an easel. This was his studio!

Kálmán gestured to a chair whose seat was covered in what looked like a pile of old sweaters. She stood there staring at it and he laughed. "Throw them to the floor, those are just rags, my dear! If it's not on my back, it's a rag." He laughed more until he began to cough, and then spit into a handkerchief he pulled from his pocket.

She sat down and he remained standing. He took a few fat grapes off the bunch and popped them into his mouth. He chewed them, spit the seeds onto the unvarnished wood floor, and then offered his visitor a couple. She politely declined, which seemed to please him. He placed the grapes on top of a dusty windowsill and admired them.

"Now, your mother said you want to know some things about art and painting? How can I help you?"

"I want to know . . ." she began, but he'd already gone over to a stack of about fifty unframed works of all sizes leaning against a wall and plucked one out, brought it over to her. It was brown ink on a thick piece of paper, finely drawn but a little bit abstract. It looked like the ruins of a bridge. She tilted it one way and then another as if that would help her understand what she was looking at. He noted her confusion and spoke, "This is an etching I did of the Danube in 1945. The Chain Bridge is destroyed, half submerged in the water. The Germans blew it up as they retreated westward to Buda in February. I was there, saw it in ruins, how sad."

"It really looked like that?"

"Yes, it was wrecked. They rebuilt it of course. Destruction leads to construction. This is one reason why it's important to document these things. We are very good at rebuilding from the ashes and forgetting that there were ashes to begin with!" He raised a finger and wagged it at her. "Remember that. The bad times must be recorded too. Not just the good ones. So we remember."

"War is terrible," Erzsi said. A black cat with a single white patch around its right eye wandered into the room, looked up at the painter, and then walked out the way it came.

"Let me show you another one," Kálmán said, going

back to the stack and flipping through until he found a small and colorful painting in a plain, black, wood frame. There were shadowy blue bombers flying in a dark and turbulent sky, while on the ground, ghostlike people in red shirts were being led away in chains.

"This one, don't ask me, it came from my imagination," he said with a shrug. "It was based on a reality I lived through, but it was more a feeling I was trying to capture than an image of something that I witnessed." He leaned forward. "That's what we artists do. Capture feelings, moods, emotions. Your dear mother told me you have been fascinated and confused by a painting in your apartment, and that she is confused, perhaps not so fascinated, by your fascination and confusion." He smiled, pleased with himself.

"Yes, that's true. Did you know Péter Szüle?" Erzsi asked.

"Szüle? So that's who this is about? Ah, yes, not directly but I know his work well. I have seen his paintings at a few exhibits. I actually understand what you mean. There was one I recall of a seated girl with a guitar resting against her white dress. The guitar was held steady by one hand, while her other hand was on some sheet music that was propped open on a high cabinet. She seemed . . . uncertain and unwilling. The painting made me feel a bit anxious for her yet also I believed that once she started to play, she would be quite masterful. It was a little bit unnerving, yet it was an attractive painting." He smiled at the memory. "Art should be an interactive experience. So: What do you feel when you look at my painting?" he asked, holding the wartime image up, hands shaking slightly.

"I feel scared, worried, upset. Disturbed," she said. And more things she could not name. She wanted him to put the painting down, but he kept it raised.

"Good. That is how I felt when I was painting it. Now, what about the painting you have at home, what do you feel when you look at that one?" He finally put the offending artwork on his lap and folded his hands on top of it.

She described the painting in detail as he nodded slowly, eyes closed, and then told him: "Intrigued. A little sad. Yet kind of hopeful."

"You might want to know more about who the woman is, why she is, how she is. I wanted to know more about the girl with the guitar when I saw that painting. That's the point though. The clues are there, it's all there in the painting. Every choice we make is intentional. Every painting is like any real-life scene—it makes you feel a certain way. If you see a baby playing in the park, you feel one thing. If you see a dog barking, you feel another. While everyone reacts a bit differently, we're all similar. We react with the same general family of emotions." He waited for her to respond but she just sat there blinking, so he continued. "The exception to the general rule is personal experience. So, for example, while most people are happy when they see a baby playing in the park—or a painting of a baby playing in the park—some might be sad, because they always wanted a child and never had one. So you see, art can bring out a general response and a very specific one. You are a curious girl, and it really bothers you not knowing what the woman is painting, it bothers you that you don't know more about her. Me, I wanted to know about the sheet music that girl was looking at. But Szüle made the music nothing more than some vague gray lines, and he did that on purpose, same as he obscured the canvas in your painting. He wanted to leave it up to us. For us, such things matter, but other people may not care one bit about the little mysteries in paintings."

"That's true. They don't care one bit. You're right."

"Now subjects like the war evoke a general reaction and are more likely to bring out some intense personal ones as well because so many of us experienced it firsthand. You see?"

She nodded but remained silent. He looked at his confused visitor and smiled. "The war," he said, stroking his chin, "your parents don't talk about it much?"

"No, not much. Especially my father. But neither one says that much. Just that things were different before the war." She suddenly wanted to go home but knew her visit was not over yet. She was thirsty but was afraid to ask for water. Maybe he made her nervous because he was not afraid to talk about bad things. Were her parents doing her a favor by shielding her from the ugly past?

"Very different. And then several years of hell happened." He gestured at the painting. "I did a series of these, but I threw the rest in the trash. I couldn't bear to look at them anymore."

"I'm glad I didn't live through that," she said.

"I am glad too. It was scarring. And then it was over; we were saved by the Russians. And here we are today. Saved." He shook his head. "It never went back to how it was before the war. It's better in the sense that nobody's bombing our city, that there are no food shortages or rounding up of Jews. But it's not how it was. If I was not such a stubborn old guy, I'd attempt to travel at least a little, get out of here and see more of Europe."

He went over to the stack and brought back a medium-sized unframed canvas and put it on her lap. It was an unfinished painting of a Russian soldier standing at attention, a very intense look on his square face, his green eyes glaring and his thin red lips tightly pursed. The face was the only part of the artwork that was complete—the uniform and the background (what looked like several other soldiers standing around in the distance) were just partly painted.

"I saw this soldier a few weeks ago here in Budapest and I decided to paint him from memory. I started it and then felt conflicted about the whole thing, so I put it aside for now. What do you feel when you look at this?"

"I feel like I am not sure what I feel when I look at that." Erzsi squinted and tried to imagine the painting in its finished state. "Kind of mixed emotions. I know I'm not supposed to like Russian soldiers, that much is clear."

He laughed. "That's basically what was going through my head when I decided to stop. But art is like journalism. It's capturing things that happen, and they are not always good things or pretty things, though we try to see beauty in everything." He paused. "I really should finish it. One day."

Her eyes wandered around the room. There were more canvases leaning against the wall under the windows, and one caught her attention. It was a small unframed watercolor of a horse drinking from a stream, so peaceful. She asked if he could show it to her, and he told her she could go and get it herself, he was tired and needed to sit. He eased himself down into a very old and dusty red velvet armchair with a grand sigh.

Erzsi liked the painting even more up close. He explained that it was one of his earliest works, from the twenties, before he was good. As she held it in her hands, Erzsi felt an intense need to have this painting, to hang it in her room. She was feeling momentarily bold; besides, her mother had given her some money to keep with her this afternoon, so she cleared her throat and announced quite loudly that she wanted to buy it, that she liked it a great deal.

He asked her to bring it over, so she stood before him in the chair and held up the painting. "You like it," he said, and then fell silent.

"How much is it?" Erzsi asked.

He said he didn't know the value. He couldn't think of a price. How could he? The cost of supplies was going up all the time, he said in his gentle voice, staring off into the distance. He simply had no idea how much it was worth. Paint was expensive, he said, so very expensive. Then he fell silent again. Erzsi took the money from her pocket and held it out for him to examine, but he brushed it away.

"No, I mustn't sell anything today. It's a Wednesday and I never sell a painting on a Wednesday," he said.

"Really?" she asked.

"On this particular Wednesday, yes. I have to be in the right frame of mind to sell. That may be why I am not wealthy, who knows."

"Well, money isn't the only important thing," Erzsi said, repeating something her mother would say.

"That's very true. But anyway, thank you for the grapes. Now perhaps you should be getting back home before I change my mind and take all your money." He laughed and then got up to show her out.

* * *

When Erzsi got home she took another look at the painting, expecting more answers to be revealed. It was the same as before. Or was it? She looked at Marta and swore she caught the hint of a smile on that face.

"Mami, why do you like this painting?" she asked.

"I like it because it reminds me of a Rembrandt. So dark and moody." And that was all she said. Whoever Rembrandt was, he was apparently an inspiration to Szüle. Erzsi wondered whether there were other artists who liked to paint tanks and soldiers and other frightening and bleak subjects. She could imagine a Szüle (or a Rembrandt?) of a Russian soldier, just a dreary soldier vaguely lit by streetlamps surrounded by a rich, deep black-red nighttime. Erzsi vowed to attempt to paint a soldier one day. Maybe the brash one in the park who made advances on Lili, from memory. She wanted to record things—important people she encountered or critical moments that happened—but for now, her drawing efforts extended only to heavily whiskered cats and fashionable dresses.

CHAPTER 9
October 22

Lili wiped the sweat from her forehead and cursed under her breath. This was not exactly what she'd pictured herself doing at age eighteen. Laying bricks! Of all the things in the world, laying bricks was probably the last thing she'd have ever imagined. Yet here she was, at a construction site in Buda, across the Danube River from home, working on building a factory with ten other girls her age or slightly older. A work brigade, as they called it. Had any of them chosen this path? No. She had no doubt. Nobody here was studying to become a bricklayer.

It was true that Lili was interested in architecture, engineering, and mathematics—but how it was decided that such interests translated to a need for technical training in bricklaying was beyond her. Perhaps the government did not want to waste a formal education on most of the youth of Hungary. No, they would rather send the majority of them to receive technical training after high school, if one could call this technical. Yes, there was something of a science to mixing the mortar, establishing the right ratio of water to cement, and then determining how much to apply between the bricks. And there was a method to properly building a wall; there were tricks for making sure the bricks were straight and evenly spaced. Beyond that, it was just labor.

It was hard to know how her parents felt about this. It wasn't as if they had any say in it, and they mostly stayed quiet, except for the few times Mrs. Molnár had decried her slightly sunburned skin. "You're roasting like a goose out in the sun!" she said, to which Lili replied, "A little sun won't kill me," when she really wanted to say, "Why can't I just sell coats with Dad?" But she knew the answer. Because right now this is what the government wants you to be doing. Laying bricks. And besides all that, she had no desire to sell coats anyway.

On this chilly October day, Lili welcomed the sun because it took the edge off the autumn air. I'm sweating and cold at the same time, she thought. Wonderful combination. She thought of a quote she'd read once from the former Soviet leader Stalin: "Education is a weapon whose effects depend on who holds it in his hands and at whom it is aimed." They were creating a weapon in her, a weapon to be used to build great factories and design them too, if things worked out. Her potential career in architecture would not be spent designing villas overlooking the Danube or elegant downtown hotels. It would be drawing up plans for factories like this one—factories whose bricks would be laid by girls the age she was now. She chuckled at that thought. Me, a weapon! But in a communist society everyone had a role, a part to play. Everyone was a weapon of the government, because everyone did what the government wanted—when, how, and where—without asking why.

Laying bricks as training for an architecture career seemed to Lili akin to being forced to tend cows or grow carrots to learn how to be a chef. But this was her reality right now. She looked around at the other girls with her. At least she was not alone, though they were not the friendliest bunch. They chattered about their boyfriends or about famous movie actors for a few minutes and then fell silent. Today, though, they were chattering about something quite different.

"I hear there's been talk of a demonstration," the bubbly redhead said to the tall brunette with the rosy cheeks.

"A demonstration? Just what we need. When, where?" Lili asked.

"Soon. The students of Budapest are going to rally in support of what's going on in Poland. It's imminent. They're going to make demands and make their voices heard. A group of students has been working hard on a list."

"What kind of demands? Fewer classes and better grades?" Lili laughed, but the others gave her a cold stare.

"It's not a joke. This is serious." The tall brunette shook her head.

"Sorry. What's going on in Poland?" Lili asked.

The redhead spoke: "Change is going on. Things are happening. There is a push for more freedom. Grab a newspaper and see for yourself."

"Well, I'm glad that someone somewhere is making progress," Lili said. "But how will expressing our solidarity with them change anything here?"

"It's okay," the brunette said. "Not everyone wants to participate or understands the need for this."

"I didn't say I wouldn't participate," Lili said without knowing what that would even entail. "I might!"

"Well, then show up tomorrow. Hundreds will come, maybe even thousands. Word is spreading. The time is ripe for change and it's up to us," the redhead said, putting down her trowel. "I'm Antonia, by the way."

"Lili, nice to officially meet you."

"And I'm Olga," the brunette said. Lili shook their hands and promised to show up downtown for the rally the next day.

CHAPTER 10
October 22

Though there were only four of them in the household, lately it seemed as if there was an honorary fifth family member—the radio. Positioned as it was in a corner of the living room, in the past the radio was often silent and forgotten for days at a time, but this fall, Mr. Molnár was prone to turning it on daily. Not that Mrs. Molnár didn't listen, but when she did it was usually to opera (mainly women singing in such high octaves it made Erzsi shiver) or folk music (like the kind Ivan played on his accordion), and always when Mr. Molnár was at work. Mr. Molnár was more likely to tune in for the news bulletins that came on every hour. Erzsi was not actually sure what was being said during these bulletins. The announcer's voice was so monotonous that whenever Erzsi tried to listen, she was immediately bored and struggled to pay much attention. Invariably, it was some announcement about the economic situation or the musings of some or other Minister of This or That who had made some formal proclamation about how well Hungarians were doing and what the future held for them.

Sometimes, Mr. Molnár preferred listening to Radio Free

Europe, which was broadcast from outside Hungary and whose signal the Soviets attempted to jam, causing occasional screeches and whistling noises. Through Radio Free Europe he could get the "real" news and a different and uncensored perspective on what was happening in his own country.

If the radio was on, Erzsi learned to quickly tune it out. There were only rare occasions when she got to listen to the radio herself, and then it was only briefly and for a children's show that was mainly dialogue between two silly puppets whom she should have outgrown by now but still enjoyed.

On this particular Monday evening, Erzsi came into the living room clutching her math homework, desperately hoping that her father could help her fill in what was still an entirely blank page. She would have asked Lili, but her sister was over at Ivan's apartment, probably listening to more accordion music, whether she wanted to or not. As the radio announcer droned on in a rapid monotone, Erzsi opened her mouth to speak but her father immediately raised a finger to his thin lips and said, "Tch-tch!" pointing at the radio. Though Mr. Molnár did enjoy listening to the news, it was not usually a mortal sin to speak during the broadcast. This time, however, he seemed completely absorbed. He gave a whistle for his wife to come in from the bedroom where she was resting; a whistle followed by her name: "Anna! Come here!"

When Anna Molnár poked her head into the living room, her husband gestured at the radio. The announcer was not even talking about events in Hungary, he was speaking about Poland. Anna came in and settled on the couch, hands folded neatly in her lap.

"The Central Committee of the Communist Party of Poland elected Gomułka as the first secretary of the Polish Communist Party yesterday at night. At the same time, it decided on the composition of the new Politburo. It does not include General Rokossovsky, who received only twenty-six votes out of seventy-five. At least fifty votes are required to be elected to the Politburo. In addition to Ochab and Gomułka, the new Politburo will include Prime Minister Cyrankiewicz . . ."

Anna looked down at her hands as the announcer listed the names of all the new Politburo members. He continued, *"Praising the decision of the Central Committee, Warsaw Radio stated that after this important decision, Poland had crossed the threshold and nothing could now stop the great turn of Polish historical development. According to a Warsaw Radio commentator, spring had arrived in Poland—in October. The main features of this Polish spring were the restoration of the honor of truth, the breaking with lies, the rehabilitation of true authorities, and the overthrow of false authorities."*

János Molnár nodded and wagged a finger at the radio as if scolding it. Then he clapped his hands together loudly, startling his wife. "False authorities! Amen! Now if we could have the same result here in Hungary." He was looking at his daughter Erzsi when he said it. She was the future—the future of the family and the future of the country. This was what change was about, after all. Not the ancient ones like himself, already almost fifty years old. Almost fifty! That number seemed impossibly high. Sure, his wife was younger, but still, they were both relics of the previous generation. Polish spring—spring was rebirth; springtime was about youth. The change that was happening in Poland and that he hoped would spread to his own country was not for him, it was for the next generation. Though he knew that most of what the announcer said was meaningless to his daughter, he hoped she understood the gist of it.

The announcer continued:

"The hope of the Polish people for the acceleration of the liberalization process is expressed in hundreds of thousands of congratulatory telegrams and resolutions in rallies. Workers and youth adopted a number of motions for resolutions at mass rallies yesterday and today, in which they welcomed the decision of the Central Committee. The flood of resolutions and letters to the Central Committee unanimously express the solidarity of the entire Polish people with the new leadership."

The words "new leadership" sent a shiver down his spine. That is what we need here, new leadership! Out with the old and in with . . . well, Nagy was not new, but he would be a welcome change. And with an exaggerated sense of what Erzsi understood, Jancsi asked his daughter, "So what do you make of all this, little one?"

"All I can say is Poland shmoland," Erzsi said with a shrug.

Jancsi shook his head gravely. "No, not quite." He tried to take on a patient tone to veil his disappointment that his daughter could not grasp the meaning of all these developments. He knew that he came across as unnecessarily gruff at times, but this time he caught himself and tried to soften his words. "What happens in Poland can happen here. We're in the same boat."

"I wish we were in a boat. I would love to be sailing right now, not a care in the world!"

"Try to be serious. This is an important development," he said. He could tell that his wife wanted to intervene and tell him he was being unreasonable. To think their young daughter would be able to engage in a discussion about the finer points of political revolution! But she kept quiet, and he continued. "Poland, Hungary, Romania . . . Yugoslavia. We're all in this same situation. The dark cloud that descended after the war floats over all of us. If one country stands strong, the others can also."

Erzsi nodded and smiled at her father, and he kissed her head. "I guess you're right. Change would be good! And we're all like teammates, like on Nadia's fencing team. If one does really well, then it's good for the whole team."

"That's one way of looking at it," Jancsi said with a raised eyebrow. "All this politics stuff can be boring, I know. So, if it takes a little creative thinking to wrap your brain around it, so be it." He thought back to when he was her age. Politics and government were far from his mind back then; he was focused on getting into endless trouble with his ragtag band of friends, knocking on neighbors' doors and then hiding, even as the Great War raged on around them. "All right, you can run along now," he told his daughter as the newsman spoke about events in London and Paris. He shut the radio off and the announcer's voice faded gradually into nothing. He'd tune in again in the morning before work to see what else had transpired in Warsaw.

Erzsi didn't move. "I said you may go, it's okay." He winked at her and gestured toward her room with his head. The poor kid was frozen in place, perhaps thinking he expected her to express more enthusiasm for political reforms. He'd have better luck talking to Lili about these things.

"But Apu, I have a homework question!" She waved the paper in his face.

"Oh, homework. Okay then, let's see what you've got."

She handed him the homework sheet. It was filled with questions about geometric shapes and equations about their measurements. "If the change in Poland . . . comes to Hungary," she started, then paused. János raised his eyebrows, excited that she was about to say something profound. Then she finished her thought: "Does that mean no more homework?"

He laughed. "Oh, Erzsi. I don't think so, but you never know. If the Anti-Homework Party takes hold, then you might be in luck." He looked down at the paper again and added, "We both might be in luck, actually."

She seemed confused at first, as if contemplating the possibility that there was such a thing as an Anti-Homework Party, but then got his joke and smiled. She leaned over and kissed his cheek, which always melted a little bit of the hardness from his face. "Well, maybe if change does come, then you won't have to work so hard anymore."

He nodded. "Yes, Erzsi. Maybe so." He didn't finish the rest of his thought out loud—that he didn't at all mind working hard so long as the reward was equal to the effort.

CHAPTER 11
October 23

Tuesday, October 23, 1956, was a particularly lovely autumn day, warmer than usual for late October. Besides the pleasant temperature, it was one of those days that start out seemingly destined to be forgotten but end up forever ingrained in memory and in the pages of history books.

That morning, Erzsi's mother, as she would recount in detail later that evening, was on Margaret Island, a recreational paradise in the Danube River, wedged between Pest and Buda. Easily reachable by tram, Margaret Island was known for its massive Palatinus water park, a complex with numerous swimming pools, including one that was once the largest in all of Europe. Aside from the pools, the island was also known for its park-like setting and its famous Grand Hotel.

Mrs. Molnár had decided to go there for a walk and some fresh air and sunshine. As she walked past the Grand Hotel around noon, Mrs. Molnár noticed a flurry of activity. A continuous stream of guests hustled with their luggage out of the hotel and into waiting taxicabs, which peeled away with a great sense of urgency. She wanted to ask someone what was going on but brushed it off. It must have been some kind of convention. The attendees were traveling together and had a train to catch.

While Mrs. Molnár was watching guests flee the hotel, Erzsi was at school as usual. The hours seemed to drag on, because her teacher was being especially spiteful, repeatedly calling on her every few minutes.

"Molnár! Pay attention!" and "Molnár! What's the answer?" and "Molnár! Why is your book closed, we are on page forty-seven!" and "Molnár, did you learn anything from your homework?"

When the bell rang, signaling day's end, the teacher asked Erzsi to stay a few minutes longer to practice some of the math equations on the board. Apparently, her father's help was not much of a help after all. He'd been distracted by the news on the radio, for sure. And now she would pay the price. Well, if she was late getting home, Mami would know why. The fall semester was young, but she'd already had detention a couple of times.

This was nonsense anyway, staying late. The teacher was not helping. She wasn't even watching, she was busy gossiping with another teacher in the hallway, leaving Erzsi struggling to work out the very same problems she and her father had both failed at, all by herself.

After a half hour of writing increasingly nonsensical equations on the board (her favorite was $a^2 + b^2 + c^2 = Me^2$), Erzsi put the nub of chalk down, grabbed her belongings, and walked out. Her teacher was nowhere to be seen. *If I get in trouble for leaving, so be it, but I'm not waiting around for nothing!*

She emerged from the building and sensed a strange kind of energy in the air. Maybe it was her imagination, but it almost seemed like there was an electricity, a buzzing, the distant sound of voices. She shrugged it off and started along the four long blocks toward home. She'd gotten only half a block when she heard her name. "Erzsi! Hey! That you? Wait up!"

It was the unmistakable voice of her boisterous cousin Pali. She turned to see him jogging toward her, an impish grin on his gaunt thirteen-year-old face. She greeted him with a meek hello and he laughed. "That's my Erzsi, shy as ever. What are you doing out here so late?"

"Blah. The teacher was unkind." To put it mildly.

"Unkind, eh?" Pali smirked. He was enrolled in an after-school program a few blocks away. "I've had many unkind teachers, but I'm a boy and I'm annoying and so that's to be expected." He laughed. "Usually they go easier on the girls, shame."

"Shame is right. Well, I'd better get home now. It was nice to see you," Erzsi said as she turned to walk away. Pali held a finger to his lips and then said, "Listen! Something's going on!"

That buzzing. The hum really was people's voices. A crowd was flowing down Sztálin Street. Pali started to walk toward the crowd and told his cousin to follow him. "But I . . ." she said.

"Listen, stick with me. Who knows what's happening; it's not safe for you to go home right now. Better that we stay together until we figure out what's going on! Cousin power, right?"

She tried to take his moist hand, but he squirmed out of her grip. Stay together, indeed! Boys. So immature. Instead, she held on to his jacket to make sure they didn't get separated. It would have been better just to head home. This was not a good idea. Around them, she could now make out what some of the voices were saying, catching snippets of conversation or yelled slogans. "Freedom!" someone shouted. A couple of college-age kids nearby kept saying the words "protest" and "revolution," which kind of frightened Erzsi. Pali, on the other hand, seemed emboldened by the growing, surging crowd. As they walked, people looked out their apartment windows and waved and applauded.

"This is exciting," Pali said. "Isn't it exciting? This could be something."

Something, indeed, but what? She thought of the conversations she'd had with Lili about change, and about the radio announcer yesterday with all the talk of Poland. Was this the something that everyone seemed to be waiting for? They appeared to be headed toward Petőfi Square, near the Danube, and fairly far from home. Mrs. Molnár's rule about her daughter exploring or wandering was "If you can see the river, you've gone too far!" Maybe Mrs. Molnár would soon head over to school to look for her daughter and then get worried.

But those thoughts were interrupted by the increasingly louder and larger crowd. They were gathering at the statue of the nineteenth-century Hungarian poet Sándor Petőfi. Pretty much everyone in Hungary knew Petőfi;

he was a national treasure. Only twenty-six when he died, Petőfi was not only a poet but also a revolutionary, and he had been killed in battle during the Hungarian Revolution of 1848. Though that revolution ultimately failed, it was a symbol of resistance and hope—and Petőfi himself was the very epitome of that spirit. Erzsi looked around. An electric sea of hundreds, maybe thousands of people surrounded the statue, onto whose base had climbed a well-known theater actor, Imre Sinkovits, who was himself just a little older than Petőfi had been when he died.

Sinkovits started to speak in a loud voice. He began to recite Petőfi's famous poem called "Nemzeti Dal," written for the 1848 Revolution:

> *Rise up, Hungarians, your country calls!*
> *This is the time, it's now or never!*
> *Should we be prisoners or free?*
> *This is the question, make your choice!*
> *Oh, god of the Hungarians,*
> *We swear,*
> *We swear to you that prisoners*
> *We shall no longer be!*

"Why is he reciting that now?" Erzsi asked her cousin.

"Shhh! He's trying to inspire the crowd. And it's working! Listen to the words. Understand them!"

Sinkovits continued:

We've been prisoners until now,
Damned lie our forefathers,
Who lived and died freely,
They cannot rest in slavery.
Oh, god of the Hungarians,
We swear,
We swear to you that prisoners
We shall no longer be!

"Inspire us to do what?" Erzsi asked. "What is going to happen?"

"Can you possibly be quiet for two seconds?" Pali asked, waving a hand at her.

"I don't think so." She loved annoying her cousin. The crowd was cheering as Sinkovits spoke, and Pali whistled his support. Erzsi clapped her hands. Someone shouted, "Russians go home!" as Sinkovits read.

The Hungarian name will be beautiful again,
Worthy of its glorious fame of old;
We must wash away the shame
Of what the centuries have done.
Oh, god of the Hungarians,
We swear,
We swear to you that prisoners
We shall no longer be!

Where our graves rise,
Our grandchildren bow down,

And in blessed prayer
Speak our holy names.
Oh, god of the Hungarians,
We swear,
We swear that prisoners
We shall no longer be!

Erzsi wished she had a pencil and some paper to sketch this scene, a sea of people riveted to the man who was reciting the words of their beloved hero. She thought of Kálmán's words—we must never forget. She wanted to draw a picture of this moment and show it to him. Or maybe he was here right now, in the crowd, recording this moment himself. She looked at her watch and realized her parents would be frantic by now, wondering what happened to her. She told Pali it was time to go, it was time for them to get home. He resisted at first but finally she convinced him that their parents would be scared and wondering where they were.

***

"What on earth were you thinking? That is what I want to know!" Mr. Molnár fumed as he clenched his fists, opened them, and clenched them again. "Things are getting bad out there. Never mind that your sister is still not home and I have no way to reach her or find her."

"Apa, don't be mad. Pali took me ..."

"Pali shmali! You did not have to go. You're just a little

kid, people get trampled in crowds. Trampled and injured or worse. I'm sure your aunt is scolding Pali right now too."

"Didn't you participate, Apa?" Erzsi knew her father had gone to work today, like any other day. He must have encountered something along the way.

"I saw the masses of people flowing along the street, and I knew something was up. But no, I didn't go along and investigate. I came home so I could listen to the news and understand what was going on. Only to find both my daughters were not home!"

Sometimes it's necessary to be the news rather than just listen to it, Erzsi thought. She didn't say that, because she was too young to say such things. If Lili had said it, she could have gotten away with it. "Go to your room and stay there until I tell you to come out!" Mr. Molnár said.

✳ ✳ ✳

She lay on her stomach on the bed, trying to capture on a sheet of white paper the scene she'd witnessed. She thought of the painter and his unfinished portrait of the soldier. All art begins with the crude and becomes refined. It all starts with a sketch, with some lines and general notions. She started with the statue of Petőfi on its raised pedestal in the center of the paper, sketching his trium-phantly raised right arm, the scroll in his left, the folds of his cloak. Then she drew the outline of the actor Sinkovits standing there reciting the poem, and added in dozens of people, shadowy masses with circles for heads and a few lines for raised arms that matched Petőfi's pose. She closed her eyes and tried to picture what was missing. The trees! She drew in a few bare branches in the background. Yes! That was it, that was the scene. Raw and abstract, but she loved it. She smiled. It was a memory captured. And no matter what else happened, she'd have this moment preserved.

CHAPTER 12
October 23

Darkness had recently fallen on this eventful Tuesday in October. At the northern end of Sztálin Street, Lili watched with a shiver as the crowd set about attacking the statue of the hated former Soviet leader Joseph Stalin. To the people of Budapest, he represented everything that was wrong with their country, he represented a hostile take-over of a nation that had its own heroes and leaders who should have had their own statues. It was Heroes' Square after all! Heroes! Whose hero was Stalin? Not mine, she thought. Not ours. Stalin belonged in Moscow, not here. The people were looking for any symbols or signs of the Soviet presence and were ready to dismantle or destroy them. She saw one young man carrying a small red metal star, the communist symbol, which he must have ripped off a building moments before. The man held it up for whoever was watching and yelled, "No more stars!" Then threw it to the ground and stomped on it, to cheers from a few people in the crowd.

But nearly everyone in the gathered mass was focused on the statue; they clearly wanted to topple Stalin, thinking it would send a loud message to their oppressors that they would not tolerate being under Soviet rule anymore.

Lili listened to the chants of "Russians go home!" and "Freedom!" and felt breathless with optimism but also petrified with fear. This was no longer a demonstration. It was the start of a revolution.

She wasn't really close enough to the action to see exactly what was going on, but it looked as if they were having some problem getting the statue to budge from its huge, high stone pedestal. Someone handed her a flyer that had sixteen numbered points listed on it. She read through them quickly.

The demands were very specific and began with: "We demand the immediate evacuation of all Soviet troops, in conformity with the provisions of the Peace Treaty." Other demands ranged from a new government under Imre Nagy, to the reorganization of Hungary's economy, complete freedom of the press and radio, higher wages for workers, and the release from imprisonment of Cardinal Mindszenty.

And then she read one of the last demands: "We demand that the statue of Stalin, symbol of Stalinist tyranny and political oppression, be removed as quickly as possible and be replaced by a monument in memory of the martyred freedom fighters of 1848–49."

In the midst of all the cheering and yelling of the throngs of people, the clattering and banging against the Stalin statue, a feeling of pride swelled in Lili's chest. There was a mix of smoke, sweat, and perfume in the air, and she inhaled it deeply. Maybe the other demands would take some doing but this one, this one was happening before her eyes. Maybe the other demands were more important for the future of the people of Hungary, but here and now, this one was symbolically the most critical. Someone was now trying to attach steel cables around Stalin's neck in an attempt to pull the statue down. There was a great roar of anticipation from the crowd, but the stubborn statue did not move.

She could remember when this monstrosity was installed here, five years before, in honor of Stalin's seventieth birthday. Nobody was happy about it or any of the other symbols of Soviet control, but nobody dared speak such things out loud. One never knew when the dreaded secret police were listening.

Lili wished her parents could be here to witness this moment. Right now, they were probably home, worrying about her. Too bad, because she was not about to miss this moment. They might be mad at her, but she'd describe the scene with such enticing detail that they'd quickly forgive her and get caught up in the wave of patriotic hope.

She'd started the afternoon among the gathered crowd near the Danube and wound up here, following the swell of people who had made their way to the Heroes Square. She'd walked right past her building along the way, and swore she saw her father looking out the window. She'd waved frantically in the hopes that he'd see her, but she was just one person in the human sea that was coursing along Sztálin Street.

Everyone wanted the statue to fall but the situation was more complex than she had imagined. The students' demands for freedom were within the context of the existing system of government. And when Lili thought about it, that was okay. She noticed that some people were actually holding up pro-communist signs. Not everybody was against communism, they were simply against the Soviet rule of Hungary. There were things about communism that they liked, but they certainly did not like being under the tight control of another country and they despised having this statue of Stalin in the middle of their beautiful city.

Just as she was thinking that the chances of anyone recognizing her seemed minuscule, she heard her name being called, loudly. At first, she thought it must be some other Lili. But the voice was insistent and persistent, and coming closer.

"Lili! Lili! Hello, turn around! It's me!"

Lili refused to turn around. What if the secret police were rounding people up one by one, their loathsome activities obscured by the sheer volume of the crowd? How could they know her name? They had files, dossiers, on thousands of Hungarians. What if one of those girls laying bricks with her the other day was a spy and had turned her in to the police! No, she was going to ignore the voice, pretend not to hear it, even though the voice did sound familiar. And then she heard it—the unmistakable sound of an accordion starting to play the Hungarian National Anthem. She whirled around to see her boyfriend just a few meters away, behind an old man and a couple of teenage boys. As soon as Ivan saw her face, he stopped playing and squeezed past a few people to embrace her.

"I never thought I'd find you here," he said.

She smiled and said, "These are strange times. Strange things happen."

"Fair enough," he said. "Are your parents here too?"

"No, they're not," she said. "I mean I don't think they are. At least, I haven't seen them here."

"But they know that you're here, right?" he asked, punctuating his question with a dramatic note on the accordion.

"Actually, no, they have no idea," she said after briefly considering lying. Lying would come back to haunt her anyway.

"Well, that's a bit reckless, isn't it?" he asked.

There were more shouts from the vicinity of the statue as the crowd renewed their attempt to topple it.

"I mean, I'm often out in the evening. I am eighteen after all."

"But on a day like today, do you think it's wise to be out without their knowing where you are? There have been gunshots fired, people have been killed."

"That's terrible," she acknowledged, "but I'm sure they know I'm fine."

"Well, in my humble opinion, you should go home now and tell them that you're fine. It looks like this will be going on for some time. You can always come back; it's not far." Leave it to Ivan to be reasonable. She sighed heavily. "And what about you, and what about your parents?"

"They know I'm here."

She looked around, absorbed the electricity in the air, and felt a renewed sense of the importance of the day. "But I don't want to miss this!"

"Looks like they're going to be at this for a while. To be honest they may never get the statue to fall. Just go home. You're not dressed for a statue toppling anyhow." He laughed and she shook her head. Such a wise guy!

"Fine. But I'll be back."

"If you can't come back, don't worry. I will fill you in on what happens."

"Well, you just make sure you're careful," Lili said, giving him a kiss on the cheek.

"Never mind me," he laughed. "I've got to protect my precious cargo here." He patted the accordion gently as if it were a cute puppy and then started playing again with dramatic flair. As Lily slowly made her way out of the crowd, she could still hear the strains of his instrument in the distance. She looked back at the statue of Stalin one more time, and then headed toward home, down the street that had been given his unwanted name.

CHAPTER 13
October 24

"People of Budapest, all those who, in the interest of avoiding further bloodshed, lay down their arms and cease fighting by 1300 hours today will be exempted from prosecution. Using all the means at our disposal, we will realize as soon as possible the systematic democratization of our country in every field of Party, State, political, and economic life. Heed our appeal, stop fighting and secure the restoration of calm and order in the interest of our people and our country."

Mr. Molnár turned the radio volume down and addressed his family. "See what Imre Nagy has to say? He's on our side. He's the prime minister again. He's trying to protect us from being killed. It's bad out there. We need to make our voices heard, but if we go too far there will be bloodshed and persecution." He folded his arms, pursed his lips, and nodded slowly.

"Doesn't exactly sound like he's on our side," said Mrs. Molnár from her favorite spot on the sofa.

"He is caught in the middle, you see? He is trying to appease the big Soviet bosses but also appeal to the people of Hungary. We should stop fighting."

"Daddy, do you always have to throw cold water on everything? Rejoice in this moment! Revolution is how change happens. Nothing will be democratized until the entire government is frightened out of their wits at how far we will go to have change," Lili said.

"Spoken like an eighteen-year-old. When you've lived through everything I have, it's hard to rejoice just yet. Cautious optimism is what I have." He turned the radio up again.

The Radio Budapest announcer was broadcasting an urgent alert: *"Women! Do not let your husbands run into deadly danger! You must prevent them from supporting counterrevolutionary forces. Mothers! Do not let your sons run into the streets, where they face deadly gun barrels."*

"They didn't say anything about daughters!" Lili said with a smirk.

Mr. Molnár shook his head. "I wish they had." He paused and added, "I would switch to Radio Free Europe, but I fear they'd be encouraging you to go and fight."

Lili sighed, went to her bedroom, and slammed the door behind her.

* * *

Erzsi's family considered themselves luckier than most, because the purveyor of the most delicious treats of all, the Friedman Wafer Company, was located in their own building, on the ground floor in the courtyard of 92 Sztálin Street. Every so often when the mood struck, Mrs. Molnár would hand Erzsi some money and send her down to get some wafers for the family to enjoy. "Here's some money. Go get us some wafers. And don't eat them all on the way back!"

"Maybe I will and maybe I won't!" She laughed as Mrs. Molnár shook her head. Mrs. Molnár knew that Erzsi did not have a great track record with bringing baked goods back home intact. Lately, there had been several times when she was sent to the market down the street to fetch a loaf of freshly baked bread, and by the time she got home, the bread had several bites taken out of it. The excuse was invariably that she had to check the bread and make sure it was acceptable, because she would not want to bring home a loaf that was not good enough for the family to consume. This excuse was met with a raised eyebrow and a not-so-stern warning. The bread was not so much an issue as the wafers, though. Everyone in the family enjoyed them and Erzsi knew if she so much as nibbled anyone else's wafer, she'd be punished.

On October 24, Mrs. Molnár gave Erzsi money to get some wafers. There was no joking or banter, just the silent hope that the shop was still open in this uncertain time. As it turned out, there was no line, so Erzsi walked right into the courtyard apartment that doubled as a wafer bakery and shop. The short and busty Mrs. Friedman, busy tidying up behind the counter, put the rag aside and seemed surprised to see one of her regular customers: "Erzsébet! Why are you out and about? It's dangerous to be outside these days!"

"I guess. But my mom sent me here to buy some sweets."

"I see." She frowned slightly in disapproval of the decision to send a child out of the apartment in the midst of turmoil, but then put on a smile again. "Well, in that case, what can I get for you today?"

"I would like four of the plain wafers with powdered sugar. Please."

She brushed some powdered sugar from her apron. "This sugar gets everywhere. One year we had an invasion of bees that forced us to close the shop all day for pest control. Anyway, yes, I think I can help you with that. I just happen to have four left right here."

"Well, that's lucky for me." A quick thought to eat all four wafers and tell Mrs. Molnár that they had run out entered Erzsi's head, but there was the small matter of accounting for the money she'd been given. Oh, well.

"Yes. Sometimes it's hard to keep up with the demand. We're just a small operation here. But . . ." Her eyes glazed over and she stared over Erzsi's head and across the courtyard.

"But what?" Erzsi took a deep breath and inhaled the sweetness of freshly baked goods. At least here in the courtyard, she did not have to think about the craziness that was going on in the rest of her city.

"We used to have a big factory. Not that long ago. We were a bakery. We had many employees and made lots of baked goods. It was a considerable operation." She sighed mightily as she wrapped the wafers in paper and tied the bundle with a piece of string. "Bread. Lots and lots of bread! Loaves upon loaves, as far as you could see and beyond. Thousands of loaves a day."

Erzsi wanted to ask what happened, but Mrs. Friedman beat her to it.

"And then came nationalization. Do you know what nationalization is?" She looked at Erzsi and smirked, shaking her head slowly while she studied Erzsi's expression. Erzsi did know what it meant, but she was having trouble putting words to the concept.

"It's the same thing that happened to your father's store." Mrs. Friedman was an occasional customer of the store. She'd bought two coats over the years. Erzsi had never heard anyone refer to something "happening" to Dad's store like that, though he often spoke of how the business had been different once. Mrs. Friedman studied Erzsi's face and nodded slowly, as if seeing something very grave. "But you're a young girl and don't need to think of such things, do you now?"

"I think of a lot of things. I'm kind of a worrier," she replied, clenching her fists.

"Oh, you sweet girl. It's true there's a lot to worry over these days. But things will get better. Though unfortunately, we are about out of flour and so we will have to shut down until everything blows over."

Erzsi handed the woman the money and received the four wafers in exchange. She was about to leave but turned back to face Mrs. Friedman. "Do you ever think of what it would be like somewhere else?"

"Well, yes, of course, we used to have a factory on Kisgömb Street. Before it was taken over by the government.

A big factory and lots of workers. There was a rule about factories and the large ones were nationalized. And what an operation it was." She frowned at her current surroundings. "But this is what it is, and for now, it's ours to own and run, not having more than a few employees. So, yes, I do think of moving into a bigger shop, just big enough that we could still own it ourselves."

Erzsi shook her head. Why did adults misunderstand her so often? "No, I mean, do you ever think of what . . . of living somewhere else? If that's a problem in this country, then what about moving away to another country, so you could make as many wafers as you want without anyone interfering?" The wafers smelled so good.

Mrs. Friedman laughed heartily until her cheeks turned red and her nostrils flared. "Oh, child, you do think of many things, don't you?"

"I do." She shrugged. It was both a fair question and an unfair one. At times when she thought of many things and her mind was a great jumble of ideas, she was accused of thinking too much. And when she focused on only one thought, she was inevitably told she needed to broaden her horizon and open her mind.

Mrs. Friedman was ready to move on, but Erzsi's gaze was steady, and there were no other customers waiting. The baker exhaled loudly and then spoke. "Many times, I've thought about that. But I always realize that I'd miss Budapest too much. So it's not realistic. Making a million wafers in, say, Italy, would not make me happy. Making a thousand here does. Anyway, who knows if people in

Italy or Austria, or wherever, would appreciate these Hungarian wafers. We'll see what comes of this rebellion. Now run along before your mother starts wondering what has become of you and your wafers! It's not so safe to be out and about these days."

CHAPTER 14
October 27

The few days that followed were emotionally exhausting and confusing. The swelling of hope could be felt across the city. The protesters, demonstrators, and marchers transformed into armed fighters—they were making their voices heard. They launched Molotov cocktails at tanks, borrowed machine guns to fire at the Soviets.

By October 28, it looked as if the Hungarian government was going to listen, to give in, to let the people be heard. It was dangerous out there on the streets, but in a hopeful kind of way. The radio was on all day and well into the night, and though Erzsi was curious about it all, she nonetheless tried to tune out the endless droning on about freedom, skirmishes, demands, policies, politics, and rebellion. Meanwhile, not a day went by that Lili didn't ask whether she could go out and join in the protesting and fighting, but Mr. and Mrs. Molnár forbade it every time.

"It's bad enough you and your sister got caught up in the events of October 23," said Mr. Molnár, but not without a hint of pride that his daughters had been part of a historic moment in Hungarian history. He spent much time looking out the windows, watching the freedom fighters running through the street. He watched the soldiers running. Most of the action took place elsewhere, but they could smell smoke and hear gunfire and shouting.

The Molnárs spent much time on the telephone with family and friends, discussing and debating the situation and wondering to each other what the outcome would be. Each person they spoke with gave a different report from their own neighborhood, from their street. Erzsi asked many, many questions, and her parents tried their best to explain things to her. It was a lot to process, so she preferred to tune much of it out. She liked to pretend that she was just on a vacation. When she wasn't playing rummy or twenty-one with Lili, she spent hours building elaborate cardhouses and playing with her wooden building blocks, making two-meter-high towers before carefully disassembling them and building more. Sometimes when there was disturbing noise from outside, she lay on the bed and covered both ears with pillows.

Life was anything but normal, and the Molnárs stayed inside as much as possible. Erzsi noticed the growing tension in the house, perhaps caused by the intensity and importance of the situation going on outside. Her parents snapped at each other constantly and Lili was very short-tempered with her sister. Their food supply was dwindling because the normal shipments were no longer able to arrive in this city under siege. And it was no longer so simple as just going to the store. There were bread lines now, and people waited for hours to get food for their families.

They knew this from the radio, from talking to their family members on the telephone, and from looking out their windows. The line for the store down the street extended almost to their building and seemed to hardly move at all. Soon enough they realized they were almost out of food and someone would have to go and stand on that bread line.

* * *

From where he was standing, Jancsi and could see only about forty people, but the line extended further than that. It was a chilly day, so everyone was bundled up in coats; as he was prone to do, he tried to see whether any of those coats happened to be from his store. He could always pick his coats out from a great distance. He just knew. *Why am I worrying about where their coats are from?* he asked himself. *I should be wondering if there is any bread left at the bakery.*

There was limited chatter among the people on line. Mostly they kept to themselves, even if they knew each other. He followed suit, trying to blend in. He just tried to keep his eyes straight ahead, focused on the back of the man in front of him. Poor workmanship in the seams. *If I made men's coats,* he thought, *I could do far better than that.* The line moved very slowly, though he did occasionally see somebody walk past with bread. He saw a woman from across the courtyard in his building, and he caught her eye for a moment, but she did not acknowledge him.

Suddenly there was a commotion coming from up ahead in the line. Jancsi saw a soldier about ten meters ahead, barking commands and accusations at someone. And then the soldier pulled out a pistol and fired at the person point blank. The sound of the shot took Jancsi's breath away, and he clutched his heart as he watched the victim's body drop to the ground, lifeless. A couple of people screamed and then another gunshot rang out; someone else on the line fell into a heap.

"Oh my God, dear God, protect me," he muttered, and lowered his head. The people on line were still and silent. The soldier laughed, shrugged, and walked away, then jumped into a waiting jeep which sped away down Sztálin Street.

By the time Jancsi had got to the spot where the atrocities had occurred, someone had covered the one body with a heavy black coat; the other body had been carried away already by a couple of friends or relatives of the deceased, sobbing as they lifted the lifeless mass and took it away. He now stood just a meter away from the high heels of the fallen woman. He didn't want to look, but he couldn't help staring. So this was what it was coming to. Innocent people being shot, for what? For nothing. Those two people went out for bread and would never return. He'd seen similar things during the war, but this was different. This felt worse. He just wanted to go home and kiss his family. But they needed the bread. He had to stay here.

A half an hour later, he finally reached the shop. They were down to their last few loaves of bread. No words were exchanged. He took the bread and left, walked slowly back home, noting that the line was just as long as before, and most of those people would go home empty-handed. He looked to the sky and thanked the Lord for keeping him safe. The sweet yeasty smell of the fresh bread made him cry. He didn't wipe his tears, he let them flow down his face as he walked.

CHAPTER 15
November 2

When Nagy announced a ceasefire on October 28, along with a new national government and the promise of the withdrawal of Soviet troops from Budapest, the Molnárs were cautiously hopeful. Still, the chaos and uncertainty of the autumn days meant life was anything but normal in Budapest. The Soviet presence was very pronounced. Despite the ceasefire, things felt very tense. No more walks in the park, no more leisurely trips to Gerbeaud Café, or even to the smaller café around the corner. There were some things, however, that had to go on as normal, in spite of everything else. The coal delivery was one of them. The entire old building at 92 Sztálin Street was powered by coal stoves, and with the days getting colder, there was no putting off a refill. Without coal, they'd freeze to death in the drafty, high-ceilinged apartment. Each of the rooms, with the exception of the kitchen and bathroom, had a coal-burning heater. The heating units were less like stoves and more like chubby grandfather clocks. They were covered in ceramic tiles that spread heat into the room as the coal burned in a compartment in the bottom center.

The stoves weren't that attractive to look at, but they were a necessity. They stayed fired up through most of the fall, winter, and early spring until it was warm enough that the air in the apartment didn't feel sharply cold on the face.

On this day in early November, when Erzsi heard Sándor calling out from the hallway, "Coal man, coal man!" she ran to the door and threw it wide open even before her mother could get up from the easy chair. But Sándor wasn't there, he was first servicing a different apartment. And then he'd have to go back out to the truck and get another sack for their place. She closed the door and waited a few minutes until she heard him call out again, his voice this time unmistakably close. Erzsi reopened the door and there he was, a short burly man with black smudges and streaks all over his pale face and in his blond hair. His gray coal sack was flung over his shoulder. His muscular, dirty arms were glistening with sweat.

"Well, hello there, Erzsi dear, how's everything with you?" His voice suited the hazards of his occupation; it was gravelly and growly. It was how Erzsi imagined coal itself would speak had it the ability.

"A little strange, I guess. Everything is strange these days." A little strange! She meant to say a lot strange but didn't want to appear frightened or overwhelmed in front of the coal man. She was relieved to see Sándor and wanted to hug him, but that would make her clothes filthy, and she'd get yelled at by both Mrs. Molnár and the coal man. Never mind that, hugging him would also make her seem like a scared little girl.

"These days indeed," he said. He scratched an itch under his nose with two fingers and got more soot on his face. "But coal is never strange, and coal does not know these days from those days. It just waits to be burned in stoves all across Hungary and all around the world, day and night, revolution or not."

"You are like the poet of coal," Erzsi said with a laugh.

"Why, yes, I suppose I am." Sándor shrugged and then sneezed mightily. "Pardon me. Curse this dust."

"Hiya, Sándor," said Mrs. Molnár, waving from the hallway. She'd been in the kitchen taking inventory of what food was left in the house.

"Mrs. Molnár." He nodded at her, then came further into the apartment, to the coal box in the entry foyer. He smelled of coal dust and sweat and cigarettes. Sándor sighed at the sight of the coal bin, opened it with one hand, and without letting the sack touch the floor, he expertly emptied its contents into the bin as Mrs. Molnár called out, "Erzsi! Stand back, it's very dusty." The sound of the coal falling into the bin was a very unique one, like hailstones on the roof of a car (something Erzsi had experienced one December a few years back and had never forgotten).

"Yeah, do as she says or you will wind up looking like old Sándor. I may as well work in a coal mine." A plume of black soot puffed from the bin as the coal was dumped in. Though he called himself old Sándor he could not have been more than thirty, thirty-five maybe, though the last time Erzsi had tried to guess someone's age, she was twenty years off, to the delight of her teacher and the amusement of her classmates.

"So how is it out there?" Mrs. Molnár asked, gesturing at the windows.

Sándor cajoled the last few pieces of coal from the sack into the bin, coughed into his sleeve, and then said: "It's not great. Everything is very tense. The bread lines are long and there are soldiers everywhere. This will be my last coal delivery for a while, the home office says it is too dangerous. You know how soldiers can be when faced with a rebellion. Impatient and unpleasant. Yesterday I saw one of them shoot someone on a bread line."

Erzsi gasped. "What? Why?" She wanted to ask if that meant shoot dead, or just injure. But she was afraid of the answer.

"No reason, I don't think. Just because." Sándor paused and squinted at Erzsi. His little eyes were too close together and almost as dark as the coal with which he dealt. "What I mean is, just because that guy was Hungarian. That's the just because. We're all targets now. For being us. When you poke a bear with a stick you don't ask why he goes on a rampage and attacks half the neighborhood."

Erzsi bit her lip. Sándor's analogy was quite unpleasant. There was an awkward silence broken only when Erzsi said, "I don't like bears much." Sándor broke into a hearty laughter that turned into an uncontrollable cough. Erzsi ran and filled a glass with water for the coal man and he drank it down eagerly. "Thank you, child. I dislike bears as well. I stay away from sticks also. So, when was the last time you were outside?"

"Two days ago," Mrs. Molnár said. She'd come into the foyer as much to be polite as to not leave her daughter alone with the coal man. "We try not to if we can avoid it." "Smart. It's dangerous. Be careful." He folded the empty sack. "I just hope this is all over soon and we can go back to normal . . . whatever that means now. Thanks to the students of Budapest for causing this mess. Not you, Erzsi. Not students your age. The older ones. You're not at fault." He laughed, and Erzsi wondered if Sándor blamed Lili for this situation.

"If you don't mind terribly, the main bedroom is almost out of coal . . ."

"Sure thing," said Sándor, though it was obvious from the way his lips pursed that he hated being asked such things. He grabbed the pail next to the coal bin and scooped some coal in, then brought the pail into the next room and filled the stove while Erzsi and her mother waited in the entry hall. "Well, this delivery should keep you going for another month," he called out. As he returned and plunked the bucket down, he added, "By then we must believe our city will be less tense. But as usual, if you need more before my scheduled return you can ring up the office, unless of course the building has been bombed to oblivion and we're all dead." He stopped and noted the mortified expressions on his customer's faces. He held up a dirty hand and lowered his head in penance. "Sorry. I tend to be dramatic. Poetic license." He laughed but the Molnárs looked at him expressionlessly. "Oh, come now. I'm sure it will all be fine. There shall be coal for everyone and old Sándor will be back next month, as much as he'd rather be retired in a cottage on the Adriatic coast. My father thinks it's going to be a bad winter, and he's usually right. Being a farmer and all, he knows things. I should have followed his footsteps instead of delving into this black hell!" Mrs. Molnár held a couple of forint coins up for Sándor to see. He bowed his head and put out his filthy hand. She dropped the coins on his palm, and he closed his thick fingers around them and thanked her with a nod. Erzsi could see that Mrs. Molnár was already cringing at the black fingerprints on the lid of the coal bin, and even as Sándor was on his way out the door, Mrs. Molnár began rubbing them away with a damp rag.

CHAPTER 16
November 5

A big, ugly, menacing Soviet tank had positioned itself right outside their building. Erzsi's parents watched in silent horror as it rolled into place, its gun angled toward their bedroom windows. They drew the curtains and ducked down, hurrying into the kitchen. It was nerve-racking just watching them pace. They spoke not a word for a few minutes, not until Lili finally said, "But why our building? Who are we?"

"We're Budapest, and we're the enemy," said Mr. Molnár in a low voice.

"So, what now?" asked Lili.

"Maybe the tank is gone already and we're worrying over nothing," said Mr. Molnár. "I'll go look." He disappeared into the bedroom and a few seconds later called back, "Nope, it's still there."

"Maybe Eisenhower will send help!" Mrs. Molnár said. "He can order thousands of troops to intervene at the snap of a finger!" She clasped her hands together as if in prayer.

"I hope. But we cannot count on anyone to intervene. The world is preoccupied with the trouble in the Suez right now," Mr. Molnár said. Erzsi knew what the Suez

Canal was but had little idea what the trouble was with it. "Hungary will be an afterthought."

There was an uncomfortable silence. Erzsi wished her father would switch on the radio, but he didn't. He just stood there, arms folded, shaking his head. She knew he was thinking, *How could this be possible—when everything seemed so hopeful?*

"So what do we do? We could go stay with my sister," Mrs. Molnár offered.

"Absolutely not! We're not abandoning our apartment. I don't care if the entire Soviet army is outside out window." Mr. Molnár pounded his right fist into his left palm and shook his head vigorously. His face was a blotchy red and his nostrils flared.

"We can't sleep in those rooms. I refuse!" Mrs. Molnár folded her arms and turned away from her husband. She knew her husband had a temper, but she was a Taurus and could be quite stubborn.

Mr. Molnár lifted his head toward the ceiling. "I suppose not." He looked at his children and his features softened. He nodded. "Okay, we'll sleep in the hall. Here." He pointed at the floor.

"Ewww. There's hardly enough room here, Apu," Lili said, disgusted.

"No, your mother's right. We can't sleep in there. We'll have to make do out here. It's almost dark. We will have to keep the lights out in those rooms. Let's not give them an easy target. Out of sight, out of mind. Come on, give me a hand with the mattresses."

One by one, they stripped the beds and then dragged the unwieldy mattresses from the bedrooms into the hallway, followed by armfuls of sheets and blankets and pillows. There was barely room to navigate around the makeshift beds to the kitchen and front door. But they would have to make do.

A speechless dinner followed, silent except for the clinking of their spoons in the soup bowls and the occasional slurp by Mr. Molnár, which was invariably met by a glare from Mrs. Molnár. When dinner was finished, the girls helped their mother clean up while Mr. Molnár listened to the announcer on the radio describe the invasion of Budapest by the Soviet army. What had seemed yesterday to be sure victory now seemed much more unlikely. The Soviet government was wary of the promised changes in Hungary, and a decision had been made to put a complete stop to Nagy's promises. Hearts were broken all across the country. Erzsi watched the hope vanish from her parents' eyes, she heard the dejection in her sister's voice, and it made her deeply sad. She lay on her stomach on the mattress and read a book for a while until her mother said it was time for bed. They took turns in the bathroom and then Erzsi stood there for a minute staring at the mattress on the floor. The same blankets that were always so cozy now looked misshapen and alien.

"Well, don't just stand there, get in," Mrs. Molnár said.

"I don't wanna," she said. Her sister was still in the bathroom. Maybe it'd feel better once Lili was here.

"The tank will probably be gone in the morning. You can do this for one night. We all can. Now come on. It's

bedtime for everyone. We need to shut all the lights off."
She stared at the bathroom door as if willing her older
daughter to be done quickly. There was something in Mrs.
Molnár's voice, a bit of breathlessness, that was disarming.
It was actually good to hear the usually unruffled woman
become a little anxious.

"Fine. But I'm not going to get any sleep."

"You have your dolly," Mrs. Molnár said.

"I'm getting too old for my Kati."

"Hmmm. Tonight you're not too old for Kati. Tonight
you're just right for her. Now in bed with you, come on."
Lili finally emerged from the bathroom and read her
mother's face and hurried into her "bed" too. Mr. and Mrs.
Molnár shut off the last of the lights and slipped into their
beds, and everyone said their good-nights.

✳ ✳ ✳

Erzsi was wrong about not being able to sleep. In fact,
she fell right asleep, slipping into a dream about Ivan,
the accordion king. In the dream it turned out that he
was actually a member of the secret police and turned in
the whole family based on something that Lili had said
to him. Thankfully, Erzsi transitioned from that dream
into a pleasant one about swimming at Lake Balaton with
her cousins last summer. And then she woke up to what
seemed like gunfire but was only her father snoring. She
was not used to hearing it at such close range. It was an
angry rumbling sound that ended with a puff of air, inces-

sant and unchanging. How did Mami sleep with this every night? Erzsi missed her bedroom. Her actual bed. The mattress on the floor was uncomfortable. She lifted the blankets off her body and sat up. There were a few distant shouts from outside, and they startled her. She stood up and looked at her sister, who was sleeping peacefully. It must be nice to be eighteen and unafraid. The distant voices faded but suddenly she heard talking, very nearby. She could make out some of the words—"orders" and "watch out"—and then the voices seemed even closer, one of them said, "Do you have a cigarette?" There was a pause and then a thank you. She wanted to wake her father, but she was afraid he'd yell at her and everyone would be awake and mad.

Erzsi stood up, clutching her doll. She waited for her eyes to adjust to the darkness then tiptoed toward the entrance to the bedroom. There was nothing further from outside. She leaned into the room. She could see the familiar glimmer of an Andrássy Street lamp through the slit between the curtains. There was something comforting about this room, maybe it was the faint scent of her sister's overly sweet floral perfume (Lili didn't like it much but Ivan did, so she obliged). She inhaled deeply. Her father's snoring became momentarily louder and then he cleared his throat. She froze until his snoring went back to its normal pattern. Her brain told her not to move, but her feet seemed to propel her anyway, toward the great window. She stood there for a few seconds, facing the drawn curtains, blinking, waiting to hear a voice. Maybe the tank was gone now. Maybe those weren't soldiers after all. Maybe they were just building tenants who were relieved to have their street back, enjoying some night air. If the tank had left, then Erzsi could wake up everyone and tell them the good news, and they'd be so happy they'd forget to scold her for going to the window. Then everyone could bring the mattresses back to their rightful places and get a good night's sleep after all! That would be delightful.

She felt the blood beating in her neck and swallowed twice, took a deep breath, and with two fingers spread the curtains ever so slightly. The tank was still there, and it looked even more ominous by night. A shiver shot through her body. At first, she didn't see the soldiers, but then she noticed one standing just to the right of the tank, using a rag to wipe the turret. The other soldier was gazing into the night sky, his back to her building, a smoldering cigarette dangling from his right hand.

Her instincts told her to close the curtains and go back to bed, but she was transfixed by this sight. It was both petrifying and comforting—seeing the soldiers as just people. The tank was just a machine that when empty was just a shell. The soldiers were no different from the one in the park that time who tried to hit on Lili. *I may be sleeping on a mattress in the hall*, she reminded herself, *but at least I can sleep*. They are on duty and will get no rest tonight. And they are far from home. She pictured the map of the Soviet Union that was tacked to the classroom wall. It was huge, spread over Europe and Asia like a puddle of ink, spreading with nobody to stop it. The Soviet Union was nothing but a gigantic stain on the world. And these two soldiers were from somewhere within that blotchy stain. Maybe they were from the same city or town or village. Maybe they lived a thousand miles apart. But they were stuck with each other now, here in this foreign place. Budapest must have seemed like an enchanted world to them. Or maybe not—this was no vacation for them; this was work. There was violence and bloodshed. Not so enchanted after all. A military jet passed overhead and snapped Erzsi out of her reverie. The smoking soldier waved at it frantically, as if the pilot could actually see him. Then he laughed and said something to his comrade but got no reply, so he shrugged and kept his gaze on the sky. Was he on the lookout for bombers? Was that a scout plane? Were the Soviets going to bomb the city until it surrendered? What a thought!

After the airplane passed, the soldier lost interest in the sky. He turned suddenly toward 92 Sztálin Street and caught sight of the girl in the window looking at him. He was startled momentarily; she looked like an apparition, lit only by the glare of the streetlamp, her black hair and pale expressionless face, lips parted, framed within an opening in thick curtains. When he realized she was a real little girl, not a ghost, he smiled and took a deep drag of his cigarette then dropped it and snuffed it out. But still, she did not move. Did she even see him? She was staring right at him, through him almost. He shivered. Then she brought a hand to her mouth, as if to stifle the noise it was about to make in her realization that she was facing

The Enemy. Yevgeny laughed. Silly girl. He called out to his mate: "Vitaly! Look, a girl in the window."

Vitaly kept on buffing the stupid tank, as he loved to do. "You polish that like it's your car," he had told Vitaly the other day, to which he replied logically, "It is, for now."

"Hey. Put your rag down and look over here. A girl."

"Is she your type? Maybe she will marry you if you ask nicely enough. Then your mama would finally stop bugging you. Though I don't know how she'd feel about a Hungarian girl. Better than nothing, I guess!" Vitaly laughed and examined his handiwork.

Yevgeny shook his head. "You moron. A little girl. Not that kind of girl."

"Fine. Show me this little girl of yours. I will be the judge."

Yevgeny turned and pointed to the window, but the curtains were completely drawn. No girl. He blinked twice. She had been there! The apartment was dark—the whole building was dark and lifeless, in fact. Vitaly cursed and spat on the ground. "You've been drinking again and I don't blame you but you have to share. It's not nice to keep such things to yourself."

"No, she was there, really." He refused to lower his arm, refused to let his finger waver, as if pointing would force the girl to return and prove him right. But she was gone, if she had ever really existed at all. It was late after all, and he was dead tired. But he had to know, he had to prove to himself that he'd seen her. "Come on, we'll go into the building and I will prove it to you!" he said.

Vitaly rolled his eyes. "We're not going into any build-ings. Now stop dreaming and keep alert for any rebels prowling the streets and looking for trouble. Not imagi-nary little girls in apartment windows!"

✳ ✳ ✳

Erzsi did not move from under her blankets until sun-light began to stream into the apartment. She'd slept only briefly, just before dawn, when her exhaustion finally overpowered the anxiety that had her staring at a jagged crack in the ceiling for hours, clutching the sheet with both hands, close to her face. In that brief time of sleep, she dreamed of playing cards with the two soldiers, at a small table in a poorly lit, ramshackle room. They were laughing with her and clearly letting her win, applauding when she had rummy and commenting quite sarcasti-cally about how she was just too good for them. Though it was not an altogether unpleasant dream, it unsettled her, and when she woke up her nightshirt was dappled with sweat. It was still early, and nobody else was awake yet. A lone bird was cheeping outside. Emboldened by the light, she got out of bed, hurried to the bedroom, and peeked very discreetly out of the curtains. The tank was still there, the soldiers nowhere to be seen. She could not shake the image of the one soldier staring at her, even after splashing her face with repeated handfuls of cold water until she could hardly catch her breath. And she would have kept going if it was not for her sister's voice calling out softly from behind the door: "Hey, hurry up in there, I need a turn!"

This plea elicited a "Shhh-shhh!" from Mr. Molnár, who was well known for his shushing, generally because he did not like loud noises. The shush was louder than Lili's voice, and now Mrs. Molnár spoke, asking what in the name of all that was holy was the matter.

"Nothing except that your daughters are being loud," Mr. Molnár said. Erzsi opened the bathroom door, face still wet.

"You look a mess and you're dripping water on the floor," Lili said. "Now get out of my way!"

Typical big sister nonsense, Erzsi thought. In that moment she decided not to say a word to anyone else about her adventure last night. What good would it do except worry everyone and get her in trouble?

***

The November days dragged on, and what seemed inconceivable at first was now just a way of life. People can get used to living under any conditions if they must. And so they got used to going outside only as necessary, sleeping in the hallway and shutting off all the lights at dark, gathering around the radio for updates every couple of hours.

CHAPTER 17
November 16

The distinct sound of a volley of bullets ricocheting off a building.

This what János Molnár heard as he walked along Sztálin Street on this chilly mid-November day. It was impossible to tell exactly where the noise was coming from, but it sounded very close, maybe just fifty meters down one of the nearby side streets. *People can be killed by stray bullets*, he reminded himself. He adjusted his fedora in response to a gust of wind that had almost blown the hat off his head and began to walk at an even quicker pace.

He'd been undecided about going to work today, but his wife's insistence that he stay home made the decision for him. He had something to prove. To himself and to her. He wasn't afraid. He'd been through much worse during the war. Everyone had. The people of Budapest were not going to hide themselves away forever. According to the news reports, hundreds of Hungarians had been killed, maybe even thousands. But now the worst was over, the rebellion had been quashed. It had looked hopeful for a few days, but once the Soviets rolled in, the end was inevitable. They simply had too much firepower at their disposal. The gunfire was probably just some soldiers doing target practice, having little else to do now that they were not battling revolutionaries.

Life must go on! People had to start emerging and resuming normal life again soon. Why couldn't he be one of the first? After all, winter was coming and the weather was getting cold. If the coal man could still make deliveries, then he could still sell coats. People needed coats and he had racks and racks of them waiting to be sold! No matter whom the profits went to, he was still proud and happy every time a customer walked away satisfied. Besides, he'd never been very good at sitting around at home. The last couple of weeks had been difficult; remaining mostly inside was torture. What was there to do that he didn't already do in the evenings after the workday—listen to the radio, read the newspaper, engage in small talk with the family? There was plenty of time for that after a full day of work. In any case he was also curious to see whether his store was intact or had been damaged. He'd heard stories of entire buildings being bombed or burned. He'd passed one abandoned apartment house that looked as if it had suffered a few volleys of tank fire; entire hunks of the facade were missing, revealing portions of a burnt-out interior. A minute later he passed the remains of a Soviet tank whose turret had imploded. Maybe some of the brave freedom fighters had been responsible for that. The Soviets had suffered casualties too, for sure. But there were so many of them, and they had so much firepower compared to the outnumbered and poorly equipped Hungarians. He knew how blatant was their disregard for human life; he'd witnessed the bread line shootings a few weeks ago. The memory of it made him shudder. It was over now, right?

He heard talking. It was a couple of armed Russian soldiers jogging down the center of Sztálin Street, paying Jancsi no mind, or so he thought. As they passed him, one looked back over his shoulder and spit, laughing as he continued on.

Okay, so things were not quite back to normal yet. The heightened military presence was going to be a fact of life for some time. He'd just have to get used to that. Should that stop him from being brave and reopening his store? Someone had to take the first step. When the citizens of Budapest peered out of their windows and saw this man in his business attire, briefcase in hand, heading to work, they might begin to venture outside.

These thoughts bounced around Jancsi's head as he continued to survey the neighborhood for damage. He passed shattered windows and bullet-hole-ridden facades, some debris in the street, a few burnt-out cars, and a wrecked military vehicle.

And then just up ahead in the middle of the sidewalk, there was a pile of garbage. Except when he got closer and realized what he was seeing, a nauseous feeling rose up from his stomach and made him woozy. It was not garbage, it was two dead bodies that had clearly been there for a few days, laying in a heap, riddled with bullets, large stains of dried blood on their coats. Their faces were ghostly pale and expressionless.

That was all.

He turned on his heel and sprinted for several blocks, back in the direction he'd come from. It was not time to emerge from hiding yet, not except for essential reasons. The city was still in the throes of the horror that had befallen it. The fighting may have been over but the trauma was still fresh. When he felt his heart pounding out of control and his breathing become labored, Jancsi stopped to catch his breath. He felt like he was going to have a heart attack. He leaned against the side of a bank until his heart slowed to a less dangerous pace. Inhaling deeply a few times, he looked up at the bare branches of an old oak tree. He knew this tree well. He knew this street well. He knew the entire city well. This, what he was seeing, was not his city. Not now. It was like the set of a war movie. It was like twelve years ago, only more shocking because it had happened so suddenly.

He put two fingers on his wrist and felt his pulse. Still slightly fast. He looked back down Sztálin Street. The bodies were not visible from here. That was a relief. Maybe he'd only imagined it. But no. The image of their faces was seared in his mind. Those were Hungarians, patriots, freedom fighters. Or maybe even just innocent bystanders who were in the wrong place. Maybe people who, like him, thought it was safe to go out, who thought they were going to be brave and set an example for everyone. A fine example indeed. He could feel the acid from his morning coffee rising up his throat. Another deep breath. He would not speak of this to his family. He'd just go home and say there was nobody on the streets, no point in opening the store if there would be no customers. There would be no customers for some time; he understood that now.

Beyond that, there was a very real chance of being detained for questioning. Perhaps even arrested. Whether an actual "crime" was committed was irrelevant. There had been an uprising and the Soviets wanted retribution. Examples had to be made so that the Hungarians would never try such a thing again. Examples could be anyone, especially a businessman walking the street on a cold November day.

He decided that running would make him seem guilty, so he walked slowly, head down, heart thudding in his chest, all the way home until he collapsed on the couch. He didn't feel like speaking, but then his young daughter approached him.

"Apu, are you okay?" she asked in her disarming way.

"I wasn't but I am." That was all he said before he turned the radio on, this time not to the news but to the classical music station, which was playing one of Mozart's piano concertos. He closed his eyes and let the music soothe him until he could no longer see the image of the dead bodies or the bombed-out buildings.

CHAPTER 18
November 20

"We have to leave, Apu. There's no use in staying. The future is elsewhere. It's bad now and at best it will only go back to what it was before the invasion. At worst there will be repression and retaliation. Who knows what could happen? I could be arrested if someone identifies me as having been at the statue." Lili paced the living room from end to end, hands behind her back, reminding Erzsi of last year's teacher, Mr. Erdős, whose nervous habits during the many tests he administered made him seem more anxious than the class.

Mr. Molnár remained seated, perched on the edge of the couch, rubbing his hands together and seeming to relish the chance to debate his daughter on this important issue. "Listen, I understand what you're saying, believe me. As a businessman, whatever that means these days, I get it. But still, it's not so simple. We can't just pack our things and take a train to Austria. The borders have been locked down. It was easier getting across at the end of October, but by now the security is pretty tight, from what I've heard. It's dangerous. Is it worth risking our lives?"

Lili looked at Erzsi sitting silently and wishing she had something to contribute. Erzsi glanced up at Marta and wondered what she'd have to say about all this. Probably nothing. Her concern lay solely with the unfinished canvas in front of her. Oh, to be that single-minded and carefree.

Anna looked at her husband and said: "Jancsi, don't forget, we're no strangers to danger. We somehow managed to live through the long and brutal world war, despite the odds."

"Mmm-hmm. Let's not speak of that," he bristled. He never wanted to speak of those days. Anytime Erzsi tried to ask about those days, her father would hold up a hand and tell her this was not a good time. Erzsi knew her mother had a point, but she didn't expect her father to acknowledge it, and she was correct. He said: "Starting over will be hard. This is a plain fact."

"Your brother did it, and things worked out fine for him," Mrs. Molnár reminded her husband. Erzsi noted that her mother was very good at reminding her father of a wide array of facts which she must have kept in a specific corner of her brain for possible future use.

"Oh sure, but that was seventeen years ago. Things are different now. And there are already lots of Hungarian refugees flooding the country."

"Then we'll go somewhere else," Lili said. "Don't be so eager to shut the door on this idea."

"*Macht nichts!* It's all the same. I've read in the papers and heard on the radio, practically anywhere you can name is getting an influx of Hungarians—Canada, Austria, Switzerland,

Australia. It will be hard starting over no matter where we go. And you realize the burden of that—starting over—falls on me, because I am the one who will have to make a living. All you people will have to do," he gestured at the rest of his family, "is get accustomed to the new surroundings."

"That's an oversimplified view of what we're going to go through. And I am willing to work, if need be," said Mrs. Molnár tentatively. She had never worked, so the concept was foreign to her.

"Me too," Lili added.

"Don't look at me," Erzsi said, covering her face with her hands. Everyone laughed.

"Oh, we'll find something suitable for you, Erzsi, don't worry. Maybe you can sell newspapers on a street corner." Mr. Molnár winked at his daughter. She smirked.

"Unlikely, but thanks for thinking of me," she said. She was not going to leave a normal childhood in this country only to be forced to work somewhere else. If between the three of them they could not support the family, then America was not as great as it was supposed to be.

"So are we decided then? We're going?" Lili tried to force the issue.

"We've decided nothing about anything." Mr. Molnár folded his arms and stared unblinking at his wife.

"Jancsi, your glasses are filthy," she said. "Clean them." He removed them, held them up to the light, then told her they were fine, and it was clearly she who needed glasses. She shrugged. Whenever he folded his arms, she had to find a way to make him move; she hated his stubborn nature. She was the Taurus, and it was her birthright to be stubborn. "I sometimes wonder if he's really a Leo," she would tell Erzsi after they bickered.

"Speaking of eyeglasses, can we please focus?" Lili was exasperated but Erzsi was mainly just amused. She felt privileged to be part of such a serious discussion, even if she was not a valued contributor.

"We're not going," Mr. Molnár said, replanting his arms across his chest.

"If you refuse to do it for yourself, then look at us," Lili pleaded. "Your children, the next generation. What future is here for us? Do it for us, if nothing else. Do you want a better life for us? At least we'd have a chance at a good career, a chance to make something of ourselves. Here nothing is certain." The sound of a vehicle backfiring echoed outside, but Lili took it for gunfire and gestured with her thumb. "Like I said."

"The next generation is who started this mess to begin with back in October," Mr. Molnár said under his breath.

"Jancsi!" Mrs. Molnár said, mortified.

"Don't 'Jancsi' me, it's true," he said.

"A revolution either succeeds or fails. You can't blame brave people for trying. In America and France it worked. Here it didn't. Maybe next time. But we can't afford to wait another ten or fifty or one hundred years." More jarring sounds echoed outside, this time closer than before, and accompanied by some shouting.

Mr. Molnár sighed heavily. Erzsi watched his chest move under his white button-down shirt as he breathed and remembered days long ago when she used to rest her head on his stomach while he sat in that very spot. As she listened to his heartbeat, he'd describe in the greatest detail the fantastical coats he planned to make for her when she was bigger—magnificent fur-lined creations that he explained down to the last ivory button. She'd close her eyes and fall asleep like that, and sometimes even dream of the coats he was depicting. She wished she could relive those moments, but she was too big, and he was more impatient these days. Would it be better to stay here, in the only home she'd ever known? It was a relief not to have a say. She'd just do whatever she was told. Stay or go. She folded her arms too, thinking perhaps one day she'd be like her father, gruff yet kind, resolute yet wishy-washy at times. Hmm. Maybe she already was like him. She smiled. No wonder she sometimes drove her mother crazy.

The silence was so lengthy that Erzsi was startled when her father spoke, saying simply: "Okay then. We'll go. In a few days' time, we'll go."

CHAPTER 19
November 23

Lili pulled up the collar of her dark gray coat and hurried around the corner. One of the coats from her father's store, of course. The whole family wore the coats made in his shop. Lili used to appreciate them more, but now that she was eighteen, she understood that they were not the most fashionable, though they were quite well tailored and functional. "Ah, but it fits very well, very well," as her father said when she hesitated in trying on this most recent coat he'd given her, now that she'd grown an inch over the summer. He tugged here and patted there, pulled the collar, tied and untied the belt (as he did with his customers too), and seemed rather pleased with his handiwork. "Look at that. It fits just right, see how I tailored it just so at the shoulders, and at the waist?" he said, even though one of his employees had made the coat. He mostly supervised them, barking out orders and pointing. "Wear it in good health!" he'd told his daughter, which did not, she was sure, mean wear it when you are secretly meeting your friend to talk about illegally escaping from Hungary! She was not supposed to talk of such things with anyone, but Tamás was one of a few people she needed to tell. He was different from most of her friends. Even from Ivan—she'd not dared mention anything to him yet. In fact, she'd not heard from him in a couple of days and was dreading telling him that she would be leaving Budapest forever. Part of her wanted to just leave without saying good-bye, because it would be easier for her, but that would be a selfish thing to do.

Of course, it would have been easier to just tell Tamás on the phone than be out and about, but she knew her parents would not have wanted her to tell anyone else they were leaving. It just so happened that they ran into each other on the bread line yesterday and since that was a terrible place to speak of escaping, she asked him to meet her today. Now she was late for the meeting, and she hoped Tamás would still be waiting there. It was not generally a good idea to hang around on the city streets these days. Show up in the wrong place at the wrong time and you might be shot dead. This was to be a quick meeting. Even though things had calmed down to some degree, it still felt very dangerous. The Soviet presence was ominous and the mood of the city was sad and sullen. It was more than a presence, it was a crackdown, the aftermath of a quashed rebellion.

It would be dark within the hour and Lili suddenly felt frightened. Thankfully, there Tamás was, leaning his string bean of a body against a brick wall, drumming his long, bony fingers. He nodded slightly when he saw her. He gnawed on the toothpick in his mouth a little more, then spit it to the ground.

"Hey. There you are Lil. I was about to leave." He tapped a finger on his watch and smiled.

"Sorry, sorry," she said, giving him a quick hug.

"Oh, it's okay. I would have waited a little longer anyway. Only 'cause you said it was important." *And only 'cause you've had a crush on me all year*, she thought. If Ivan knew, he'd have smashed his treasured accordion right over the poet's head.

"It was. I mean, it is." Lili was nervous. Maybe they were being watched. She embraced her friend again and whispered in his ear. "We're going to leave Hungary. Escape across the border to Austria. In a day or two from now. I just wanted you to know. I wanted to say good-bye. But you can't tell anyone."

Without hesitation, Tamás said, "I'm coming with you."

Lili withdrew from the hug. She was sure he'd be shocked and even appalled, not interested. "What? You can't be serious. You're enrolled in college."

"Look, if I stay, I'm going to be forced to study agriculture."

"Is it that bad?"

"How's the bricklaying going for you?" he asked with a smirk.

"Hey now, that's not fair."

"All's fair in love and war, my dear," he said, shooing a bug away from his neck.

"My leaving has nothing to do with bricks."

"Maybe not, but it will get you far away from them. And I want to be far away from goats and chickens and wheat and barley."

"Goats and barley don't mean you can't still write poetry."

"True, many of our greatest poets have been inspired by growing wheat, oats, and barley. Who can forget Petőfi's famous lines: 'Oh endless fields of grain, receiving too much rain, it's weighing on my brain, the soil it needs to drain! Thank God for farming school, it's such a useful tool, I've learned to train a mule, without looking a fool.'"

"Very funny." Tamás was maddeningly sarcastic. It was almost an attractive quality about him. Almost. "Well, you may not be able to make a living from poetry," she said looking into his large, expressive brown eyes. He did have the face of a poet, not just the eyes but also the jutting chin, high cheekbones, and slightly unruly hair. He was only eighteen, but he already acted like the middle-aged literature professor he wanted badly to become.

"Maybe so," he said, not believing it for a moment. "But I would rather study poetry in college and then become a farmer because I failed, instead of not even trying at all."

A chilly wind blew through the alley and Lili shivered. In the distance she could hear soldiers' voices. Or maybe it was just a couple of drunks wandering home after a few post-work drinks. This was her home. As crazy as things were now, it was her home, the only place she'd ever known. How could she leave? She realized that she wanted to stay in Hungary as much as her friend wanted to leave, and that thought almost made her cry. There was no changing his mind. Before she could speak, he continued. "So, can I come with you or not? I'll still go on my own, even if you say no."

"Better together, I guess, than to leave a helpless poet

on his own?" Lili said. Standing there against the wall, he looked anything but helpless. He looked quite together.

"Actually," he said in a hushed tone. "Not so helpless at all." He leaned forward and smiled into her face. "I have a contact." She could smell his slightly sour breath. For an instant she thought he was going to try to kiss her, but he pulled away and held his chin up high.

"A contact?"

"A guide. At the border. There's a guy who the cousin of my ex-girlfriend knows. Or is it the step-uncle of her brother? I can't recall. In any case, he could help us get across. You can't just walk across, you know. You need assistance. Unless you already have your own contact, perhaps a friend of one of your ex-boyfriends' cousins or great-aunts." Tamás took another toothpick from his inner jacket pocket and gnawed on it. There was the hint of a grin on his lips.

"A contact, eh? That sounds . . . helpful. Hmmm. I'll have to ask my parents. It's not just up to me." Adding a person to their group might complicate what had already been a torturous decision.

"That's good, I'm sure they will say yes. Your parents will like having a little extra help at the border. And anyway, your mother loves me."

Lili laughed then covered her mouth and glanced behind her. Thankfully, there was nobody around. "She tolerates you. Just barely."

"There is much to be said for tolerance," Tamás said with a grin.

* * *

When Lili got home her parents were pacing outside the front door. Mrs. Molnár was almost hysterical and ran to her daughter and hugged her tightly. Lili was overwhelmed by her mother's strong floral perfume. She tended to douse herself in it when she was nervous, to cover the sweat she imagined was repulsive to everyone around her.

"You can't disappear like that. Not these days!"

"I told you I had to run out." She did. Though without being specific as to where she was headed and for what purpose.

"It's been over an hour, and it's almost dark now." Mrs. Molnár raised her hands to the ceiling. "That's not running out, that's more than running out. The streets are thick with soldiers looking for people to arrest or shoot!" Though Lili had the same exact fears when she was standing there talking to her friend, the words seemed preposterous coming from the mouth of her mother. Her mother gave a her a look of sheer disbelief and muttered, "Jesus, Mary, and Joseph!"

Lili knew that when the holy trio were invoked, she was in trouble. But this time her father swooped in and saved her. "It's okay, Anna. Let her be. She's here now and I'm sure she had an important reason to be out. Right, Lili?"

"Yes." The good thing was she could skip the part about saying good-bye to Tamás and just address the meat of the matter. "I told my friend—Tamás—that we are leaving."

"Hey, hey! Shhhh! Not so loud!" Mr. Molnár said, glancing around. Mrs. Esterházy, the hunched old woman across the courtyard, was hanging laundry on a clothesline but she was too deaf to have heard anything, and unlikely to be a government spy anyway. Though one never knew these days. He ushered them back into the apartment and closed and locked the door.

"I thought we were not going to spread this news around or I would have told Margit," Erzsi said. "She's my best friend! She needs to know."

"No telling Margit!" Mr. Molnár said, then turned his attention to Lili: "And Erzsi's right, we were not supposed to be letting the world know. Do you realize how dangerous that is? How well do we really know this guy? He could be telling the secret police right now, about our plans."

"No, it's fine. We can trust him. Mami has met him. And in fact, he wants to come with us!"

"It's bad enough you told him, now you're recruiting people to escape with us? Out of the question!" Mr. Molnár said. He shook his head vehemently.

"I did no such thing. He volunteered it. And he has a contact. He knows someone. A guide. At the border. Who can get us across safely."

"Tamás, the foolish poet? That Tamás? The one who has no job, chews on toothpicks all day, and spouts corny verses, imagining himself to be Shakespeare? The coal man writes better poetry." Mrs. Molnár was ever practical, having married the richest (and most persistent, according to her stories) suitor. Jancsi had impressed her with the overwhelming expression of his love and devotion in the form of flowers and flattery. And the not-so-subtle description of his family's many assets. Wealthy, but not anymore, and soon-to-be downright poor once they left everything behind. She sighed.

"Wait, let her finish," Mr. Molnár said, holding a hand up. "A contact, really? I guess I thought we'd figure that out when we got there, but it would be helpful if there was someone waiting who we could count on."

"Yeah, it's for real. It's his girlfriend's uncle or his uncle's girlfriend or something like that. If it's a yes, then I just have to call him and discreetly tell him when and where to meet us, and when we get to the border, he'll lead us to his contact and get us through." Even as Lili spoke these words, she felt some of her mother's doubt nag at her. After all, it was Tamás. But a contact is a contact. It's not as if he'll be leading us across himself—it's someone he knows. Even foolish and scattershot people know dependable ones. Right?

"And did he tell you what the price would be for those services his contact was offering?"

"No, he didn't, but I assume it will not be free."

"Let me think it over for a while," Mr. Molnár said. When he said such things, it was usually the death knell for whatever proposition was being offered. But this time it took him only thirty minutes to announce his decision, after consulting with Mrs. Molnár in hushed tones in their bedroom—yes, they would allow Tamás to go with them.

CHAPTER 20
November 28

Anna Molnár paused before going into her daughters' bedroom. Lili was already done packing (if it even could be called that, considering how few things they were able to bring), and was currently sitting on the sofa reading a fashion magazine, but Erzsi was taking her time. Way too much time. This decision they'd made to leave Hungary was unnerving, for sure, but self-preservation was nothing new to Anna. How many times during the war had she made difficult choices to save herself and her family from danger? How much discomfort had she endured back then, in order to survive? It may have been eleven years ago, but once you've had to live through that, you don't forget. There are times when all that matters is living. And from everything her instincts could tell her—she tried to tune out everyone else's opinions at critical moments and just listen to her gut—staying here would not be living. Whenever the immediate terror was over, the resulting life would not be good. Insurrection was generally not greeted with open arms by occupiers like the Soviets. It was sad and ironic that those who had beaten back the enemy were now themselves the enemy. After this was over there would be retribution and further crackdowns on freedoms. And though her cousins and aunts and uncles were not planning to leave, that was their choice, and they would have to withstand whatever was to come on their own. This was her choice. Their choice. To leave.

Leaving meant not only leaving the apartment itself. It also meant leaving behind everything they owned. Paintings, furniture, décor, silverware and dishes, wine glasses, crystal vases, rugs, books, record albums, photo albums, most of their clothes and shoes—it was all to be abandoned. Well, not entirely abandoned, because Anna's niece and nephew would salvage many of these possessions; they'd already been instructed to come here when it was safe, and rescue some of the things. The paintings and photos, especially. Though the painting that Erzsi was obsessed with, that would be a bit of a challenge, what with its size. But Anna could not concern herself with such details now. The first priority was getting the family safely to Austria. She thought again of the rest of her family, and how they had no interest in escaping Hungary. They were either frightened at the danger of fleeing or hopeful things would soon be better (or at least return to the pre-revolution "normal"). Maybe the rest of the family was right to stay? Only time would tell. A dizzy spell came over her and she braced herself against the doorway until it passed.

She called her daughter's name softly, but there was no response. Erzsi was a thinker and a worrier, prone to getting lost in her own doubts. In that regard she was nothing like her mother. More like her father, actually. But so what? That was how she was. *Chacun à sa façon,* as her French teacher used to say. To each his own. She called out more sternly, "Erzsi!" but nothing. She peeked into the room to see her daughter standing in front of her dresser, empty knapsack dangling from her hand. Erzsi was growing up. She was no longer the little child who used to cling to her mother's skirt in the department store. She was within reach of her teenage years now—jewelry, boys, perfume, makeup—it was all just around the bend. Except this daughter would experience adolescence in America. She would be an American teenager, dating American boys! Oof! What a thought. Erzsi would listen to that Elvis Presley instead of Franz Liszt and Béla Bartók. It would be a mother's solemn duty to make sure her younger daughter didn't forget the language, food, music, and culture of her native land. She could not rely on her husband to do it; she already knew this—he would immediately set himself on the task of supporting the family and would have little time for keeping Erzsi grounded in all things Hungarian. One of the first purchases to be made would have to be a record player and a few albums of Czárdás music and folk songs to replace the ones they were leaving behind, and that would be as much for herself as for her daughter. It was either that or a radio, which would be doubtless be playing that new American rock-and-roll music.

She started singing softly, in almost a whisper:

They are beautiful
They are beautiful
Those whose eyes are blue
Whose eyes are blue

She peered into the bedroom again to see if her gentle serenade had any effect, but apparently not; Erzsi was seemingly hypnotized, staring dumbly at the old wooden dresser that had belonged to her grandmother.

✳ ✳ ✳

The left brass handle of the top dresser drawer had a spot of cherry-red nail polish on it, thanks to Lili. It was just the slightest spot and nobody else had ever said a word about it, but Erzsi had seen it happen. Her sister had been standing at the dresser staring into the mirror while doing her nails and a drip had landed on the drawer pull. Erzsi ran her finger over the red spot and sighed. She had the urge to unscrew the handle and take it with her, one small piece of her home, but was that really a good idea?

She still was not clear on exactly how much she was allowed to bring with her. Mami had said a few essential things. *What did that even mean?* she wondered. *Isn't everything I have essential, or why would I have it to begin with?*

A few seconds later, her mother entered the room, her shoes click-clacking on the wood floor. Mrs. Molnár always preferred to wear shoes around the house; slippers were only for the minutes leading up to bedtime. "Erzsi!

You have not packed anything. You're just standing here in a trance. Come on. We don't have much time."

"I will need a suitcase for my all my clothes," she said very matter-of-factly. It was worth a try. How could she leave all these clothes behind? The pink sweater! The green shorts! So many beloved items.

"You will have no such thing! We've been through this already. You can bring two pairs of pants and two shirts, and an extra sweater. And your doll if you want. Maybe a book, the one you're in the middle of reading. That's it. We can't be bogged down with things or we will look mighty suspicious on the train. They're on the lookout for people like us, believe it."

People like us! Mother and daughter were silent for a minute. Erzsi's back was turned to her mother, but she could feel Mrs. Molnár's piercing gaze burning her back. "Mami, are you going to stare at me until I pick out my things?"

"Yes, that sounds like a plan." She drummed her fingernails on the door to remind Erzsi of her presence. Erzsi shook her head and opened the drawer. She pulled out her favorite pair of pants, navy blue corduroys, and a pink floral-print top. "This and this, for starters," she said, stuffing them in her knapsack, identical to the knapsacks the rest of her family were bringing—they were cheap tan canvas backpacks that Mrs. Molnár had bought from a street vendor last year for use on a summer weekend at Lake Balaton. They had a nice set of expensive leather luggage, which would, of course, have to stay behind.

"Terrific, now finish up so we can go, before your father has a stroke. You know he can be impatient." This was true, but Mrs. Molnár could be equally impatient. It was typical, though, for people to project their own features and faults onto others, according to Erzsi's teacher, who liked to tell her students that they were impatient as she berated them for not finishing their classwork quickly enough.

Lili was already in the living room, waiting. Mr. Molnár was actually not ready yet; he was checking for any portable valuables he may have forgotten; Mrs. Molnár had already taken all her most valuable jewelry, including the diamond tennis bracelet that Mr. Molnár had given her when she gave birth to Lili; last night she'd spent a few minutes sewing it into the lining of her coat.

"Ah, my old watch that was hiding in the desk drawer, almost forgot this!" he called out. "It doesn't work anymore but I'll get it fixed in America. Or maybe sell it. It's worth something!"

Erzsi grabbed her doll from the bed. "All right, Kati, let's go." She tried not to make eye contact with Kati before putting her into the knapsack. She didn't want to take the doll with her, yet she couldn't leave it behind. Then she remembered—the sketch of the rally at the statue! It was on top of the dresser, folded into quarters. She shoved it in her back pocket.

"Okay, are we ready?" Mr. Molnár called. "Erzsébet! Come on. We have a train to catch."

"Give me one minute, okay?" Erzsi yelled with such force that her father did not dare argue. Either that or she was in for a smack on her behind when she got to the living room. Whatever. She took a last look around the bedroom and could not let herself believe this was it. We'll be back soon. This is only temporary, she told herself. Most things in life are temporary, cyclical. The seasons, the days of the week, sickness, school, holidays, all of them come and go and come again. So, too, this episode would come and go. By the time we get to the border, things will have calmed down, the Soviets will have left, and Dad will decide to return to Budapest. The apartment will be just as we left it. No harm done. Just an ugly little adventure. She nodded slowly in approval at her predicted fairy-tale ending, then turned and walked out of her bedroom.

CHAPTER 21
November 28

The train ride was uneventful for the first hour, but Erzsi was very nervous. They'd literally picked up and left their home. She was nervous enough as it was without the rocking of the train. As they pulled into Győr station, her stomach was churning badly. She knew they weren't at their destination, but she asked her father anyway. He smiled and told her no, it would be a little while longer. When the train came to a stop, two policemen entered their train car at the far end. They started asking to see everyone's travel documents. It was illegal to go to the border town of Sopron without papers authorizing such travel. Papers they did not have. Mr. Molnár whispered, "Okay, everyone, we're getting off here."

"What? Why?" Lili asked. She'd been sleeping and was rubbing her eyes.

"Because we have arrived!" Tamás said cheerily. While the rest of them had been tense and mostly silent during the ride, he'd maintained an upbeat demeanor the whole time.

"Shhh. Off now!" her father said, gesturing with his

head at the policemen at the other end of the car, currently preoccupied with questioning the authenticity of an old man's papers a few rows away. The family quickly got up and made their way to the doors at their end of the train car.

"I have an idea," he said when they were on the platform. They watched through the train windows as the police continued to make their way through the rest of that train car. "Okay, now, hurry, back on the train. Get on the previous car. They've already been through that car!" Mr. Molnár said, just as the announcement came through the station speakers: "Last call for the train to Sopron. Last call!"

* * *

About an hour later, the train arrived at the border town of Sopron, and they made their way off along with several other people whom Erzsi imagined were also going to make an attempt to cross the border. Maybe some of them had travel papers, maybe some had bribed the police. It was impossible to tell. But there were definitely other refugees on board. They'd made small talk with another family on the ride from Győr, the fathers delighting in the "fact" that both families were coincidentally going to visit an uncle in Sopron. When the train came to a halt, Mr. Molnár wished his counterpart good luck and the man nodded and said with a wink, "Same to you. Maybe we'll cross paths again somewhere far, far away."

Erzsi stretched mightily on the platform, even though she'd not been sitting that long. It only felt that way. Another train was about to depart the station, and some last-minute passengers hurried on. Sopron was known as the Jewel Box of Hungary. It was a place she'd heard about but never been until now. For a moment Erzsi pretended this was a just a fun day trip with her family to see the sights, to walk the streets of the old town, maybe do a little window-shopping and then return to their apartment in Budapest after a nice dinner. The brief fantasy was burst by her father snapping at Tamás: "All right, where's your friend, the contact? Is he meeting us here?"

"Here? No! This is too dangerous. Big town, the place will be swarming with soldiers. My contact is in Kópháza. A little village about two kilometers southeast of here." There would be no pleasant walk through town.

Erzsi braced herself. She knew how her father reacted to situations he was not expecting.

"Why didn't you mention this inconvenient fact earlier?" he huffed.

"Precisely because it is an inconvenient fact. You might have balked if I'd told you this before we left. So now we're here and we're close to our goal, it's just one more step we have to take. We will walk there and try to make light conversation with each other along the way. If anyone asks us what we're doing, we just say we're visiting your uncle's farm." Tamás smiled and everyone laughed. He did have a way of easing tension and Erzsi was glad he was with them.

***

After a twenty-minute walk, mostly along dirt roads, with packs strapped securely to their backs and Mr. Molnár occasionally muttering under his breath, they arrived in the village of Kópháza, right near the border. Erzsi had seen villages like this before. They were an integral part of the rural landscape of Hungary, one looking very much like the next—picturesque white cottages and sprawling farms, wide-open fields, idle plows waiting for the next season, cows, horses, and colorful flowers. Tamás led them to a small, unassuming wood cottage with a large blue letter *A* on the gray front door. The curtains were drawn but there was light coming from inside. Tamás knocked five times, then once, and then another three. This was the knock he'd been instructed to use, and after a minute, the door opened tentatively. A tall bony man with a receding hairline and a big blond handlebar mustache stood there, looked over the shoulders of the new arrivals, then nodded. "Okay, come in," he said in a hearty voice, gesturing with his big, hairy hand.

The five refugees filed into the little house. The first room had a couple of sofas and a table, and an old wood rocking chair. Erzsi noticed a few large, cheery landscape paintings hanging on the walls. After conferring with Mustache Man, Mr. Molnár directed his younger daughter to sit on the couch nearest the door and wait. The rest of them followed Mustache into the second room, where many loud voices were conversing.

She sat, back stiff with fear, and tried to hear what was being said. She could make out Mustache introducing himself to the new arrivals—he told them to call him László but admitted that was not his real name. It would be too dangerous for anyone to know his identity. He loudly introduced the Molnárs to whoever else was in the back room simply by saying, "Give a welcome to this lovely family from Budapest."

There was some hushed talking and then his voice boomed again. "Drinks?" László could be heard asking. "Would anyone like a drink while we discuss . . . payment? I accept cash, jewelry, and any other trinkets you might have of value."

"Drinks? You mean alcohol? Aren't we about to go running through the woods?" Erzsi heard her mother ask.

"Oh, yes, we are. And some folks I escort want a little something to steel their nerves. But some don't. I can pour you a club soda. And don't worry, it's included in the price of the crossing."

Cigar and cigarette smoke mingled and wafted out into Erzsi's waiting room, making her cough. The smoky stench mixed with a stale, sweet smell that emanated from the sofa. She bounced her right leg rapidly, then her left leg, and then started biting her fingernails. One of the paintings on the wall was of the Parliament in Budapest, and she studied its details in an effort to calm herself down. The building was pretty interesting, actually, when seen in its entirety from a distance. Too bad she was only noticing it now, when she might never see it again in person.

There was laughter and loud talking now, other voices. Several people were talking at once and she could not make out anything. Lili came out finally and sat next to her sister. Erzsi sighed.

"What on earth is going on in there?" she asked her older sister.

"Oh. They had to negotiate the price for going across. You know. László will be our guide. He'll get us across the border. Apa is giving him money and some jewelry right now. And he asked me to see if you want anything to drink."

"Jewelry? I hope it's not Mami's pearl necklace she said I could have one day when I'm bigger." Erzsi's mouth felt dry from all the smoke, so she asked for water. Lili nodded and a minute later came back with a frosted glass beer stein filled with room-temperature water, which Erzsi gulped down quickly after Lili disappeared again.

It was only minutes that passed, but it felt more like days. She kept looking at the empty beer stein and thinking maybe she should not have drunk so much. It would be a bad idea to try to cross the border with a full bladder. She got up off the couch and ventured into the next room. There were at least twelve people crammed in there. Her parents were against the far wall, each holding a glass of something, talking quietly to each other. Her sister and the poet were talking to a young couple on the other side of the room. László was holding court in the center of the room, telling a story to several other men of various ages who, upon closer examination, looked to be three adult brothers and their white-haired father. László stopped his story when he noticed Erzsi standing at the entrance looking bewildered.

"Oh, hang on, what do we have here? You may want to wait out there . . ." he began. By this time, Erzsi's parents had noticed and Mr. Molnár was shaking his head. But before he could make his way to his daughter to drag her back into the anteroom, László had stood on a rickety chair, cleared his throat, and had begun to speak again. His mustache glistened under the harsh lights of naked bulbs hanging from the ceiling. He looked at Erzsi and smiled. "No, never mind, it's okay. Better everyone is here now. I believe all the accounts are settled and we are just about ready. The sun has already set, but we will wait a little longer. We go by cover of darkness. We leave in half an hour! You'll all follow me. We will go across the field and through the woods right in back of this house. They lead straight to Austria. And that's that."

Tamás called out: "Hey, wait a minute. What do you mean—all? I thought you were taking us as a separate group."

"These trips are . . ." he looked at Erzsi and rethought his wording, "not so simple; it would be foolish of me to take only a few people at a time. The fewer trips the better! Anyway, safety in numbers, right?"

"A few things," he continued. "You might see searchlights. Avoid them. You might hear gunfire. Try to ignore it. Keep low and go quickly, no noise and no talking." László was counting the points on his fingers to make sure he didn't miss any. Satisfied with his speech, he scratched just above his mustache and got down off the chair, but a moment later he'd climbed back up. "And remember, once I get you close, you're no longer my problem. You're Austria's problem!" He smiled and held up his stein. "Cheers!" Nobody reacted. He paused, nodded slowly as if this kind of reaction had happened before, then decided to say more. "Don't get me wrong, my friends! I am just as much a believer in the cause as all of you. But I have a job to do. This is my part, and I take it seriously. Once you are across, I have to worry about the next group and the next. It's a lot on my shoulders, but I bear it happily to help my fellow Hungarians find a better life." A few people, the Molnárs included, gave László some applause and he dismounted from the chair and then disappeared from sight.

By now, Mr. Molnár had made his way to his daughter's side and was ready to escort her back to the other room. "Daddy, I need to go to the bathroom," she said.

Her father sighed, told her to stay put, and went off to find László. A minute later he returned. "There's not exactly a bathroom. It's an outhouse. In the back. Just go around the side and walk straight back; you'll see a little shed with a door. There's no . . . it's not like a bathroom. But when you get there. You just . . . you know, go."

János Molnár was terrible at explaining anything that made him uncomfortable. He could give a detailed twenty-minute dissertation on how to cut an intricate coat pattern out of wool and then stitch it together, but this was uncharted territory. Outhouse! Back in Budapest such things were unheard of. Of course, as a small child, he had to use one, living in the little cottage outside the city. But once his father started the store and had money, that was the last he'd seen of outhouses.

Erzsi just stood there, blinking at her father. He did not know what else to do, so he added: "In America, they have plenty of bathrooms, don't worry." He forced a smile, hoping what he said was actually a truth, and looked at the door, hoping she'd go. There was nothing but silence for a whole minute.

Finally, she said: "You come with me, Apa."

"All right then. Very well." He took her hand and together they ventured outside. The outhouse was further away than László had described, and it smelled awful.

"What am I supposed to do here?" She put her hand over her nose as she peered into the dark outhouse.

"You just . . . do what you have to. It's what passes for a toilet in the countryside."

"How do I . . . flush?"

"You don't flush, you just . . . go. I'll be right here waiting for you."

She made a face and then went inside and shut the door. While he waited, he looked at the woods, just a few paces behind the outhouse. Was this really a good idea? What exactly would happen to them when they got across with almost nothing except for a few possessions? He felt bad that there was no real plan, but what else could be done? He'd contact his brother once they got to Austria. There was no other way. This was not a vacation; it was a secret escape. It was not possible to announce their intent ahead of time, to anyone other than in person; phone calls could be tapped and mail could be intercepted. He tried to listen for any noise coming from the forest, but it was silent. Good! Maybe this was a lot safer than he'd imagined. The Hungarian-Austrian border was 320 kilometers long. Surely the Soviets could not be patrolling every inch of that, day after day, night after night? Thousands had already escaped. This would go well, he told himself. It had to.

Erzsi emerged from the bathroom holding her nose. "Let's get out of here, Daddy. That was so disgusting. Yuck!" She coughed and then filled her lungs with a few deep breaths of the fresh evening air.

He laughed and took her hand. They walked a little bit and then he said, "So, are you ready for this, Erzsi?"

"I guess so," she said. She looked down at the grass. "I mean, maybe not. I don't want to leave, not really."

"Me neither. But we have no choice. Staying isn't . . ." His voice trailed off. What could he say, really?

"But how come Nagymama is staying? And my cousins? And your sisters? And Mami's sister?" She pictured her grandma, cane in hand, smiling broadly. She knew she'd miss Nagymama greatly.

Jancsi had prepared himself for these questions. He tried to keep his voice down after he heard a rustle from the woods. "Well, your grandmother is seventy and would not do well starting over at that age in a new place. I even asked her a few weeks ago if she would ever entertain leaving Hungary, and she said no. As for my sisters, and your cousins, and the rest of Budapest, everyone has to make their own decision about this. Your cousin Nadia is heading off to the Olympics soon, so her parents want to stay put in the meantime. We just have not had the time or opportunity to talk to everyone in the family about this. It's possible others will eventually join us in America. I just don't know. But I suspect not."

"But I don't understand why? If it's so bad, then why wouldn't they want to come too? Why doesn't everyone just leave?"

This was harder than he'd thought. He stroked his chin and looked up at the dark sky. "Remember last week when you cut your finger?" There had been a broken glass in the sink, and Erzsi had reached in to wash a dish without realizing. It seemed like the blood would never stop flowing. He'd felt a little queasy seeing all that blood, but she was just fine.

"Yeah." She held up the finger and looked at the scar, nodded in approval at how it had healed.

"And remember that I was proud of you for being so brave?" He'd always imagined he'd have at least one boy, never thought he'd be the father to two girls. But as he watched them grow, he realized all that mattered was that they were hearty souls, brave and strong. And they were.

"Yes. It didn't hurt that badly. I mean it hurt. But not that much."

"And you didn't even want a bandage on it, but I convinced you to?"

"That's right."

"For you it didn't hurt and you didn't need a bandage, 'cause you were brave and didn't focus on the pain, or just didn't feel pain. But someone else might have had the same cut and cried their eyes out and felt faint and needed it to be wrapped up. So, it's like that here too. For some people, like my sisters, this cut doesn't hurt enough to do anything. For people like us, life here is like a cut that hurts badly and needs to be fixed. And we are going to fix it tonight. This is our bandage."

"So, wait a minute, are you saying we're not brave?"

He sighed heavily. His analogy, though well-intentioned, didn't really make sense. Were those who remained behind actually brave, though? Or were they just foolish? He wanted to offer some kind of answer, but he did not feel like saying more. "Never mind. Come on, let's go back inside and await László's instructions."

CHAPTER 22
November 28

After hurrying across the open field lit by the moon, the group of thirteen stood shivering at the woods' edge waiting quietly as László listened to the sounds of the night, his eyes rolling up toward the dark sky as he tried to figure out how far away were the faint voices in the woods. It was not that cold out, but the little cottage was toasty, and they were all feeling the contrast. While she waited, Erzsi took off her backpack and opened it. She pulled out her doll and looked at it. What a raggedy old memento. She thought about leaving it behind then decided instead to carry it with her through the woods, in her hand. *I'm a child here, but when I get to Austria, I won't be anymore.* She held the doll close to her chest and whispered, "We're going on an adventure, Kati!"

László turned to face the group and rubbed his big hands together. "Remember," he said softly. "I lead. You follow close but not too close together. I've had people trip on each other. Leave a few feet between you. No holding hands either. That's dangerous—one falls, the other falls too." Erzsi pulled her hat down low on her head. It was the pale blue one her grandma had crocheted for her last winter, and she loved it. He turned toward the woods again, cocked his head, then nodded. He held out an arm and counted down from three with his fingers, and then proceeded. The family of men and the young couple went first, then Erzsi's parents and Lili.

The first hundred meters were uneventful. László pushed forward, weaving between the young trees, intermittently signaling with his hands for them to keep up with him. "Above all, be quiet. If you make noise, you're not just putting your own lives at risk, you're putting mine at risk, and that's my main concern!" he'd repeated before they left the cottage, but Erzsi wondered how she was supposed to keep quiet when the leaves and twigs on the forest floor crunched under her feet. It was not quiet at all, it sounded exactly like what it was—a group of people crossing through a forest.

Now she could hear male voices talking, distant yet still a little too close. And occasional popping noises that startled her. Were they gunshots? Were people getting shot?

"Everyone, down on the ground, now!" László whispered. They all dropped to the ground, on their stomachs. After a minute or two, their guide popped his head up and signaled they could proceed on. Erzsi brushed herself off and started walking again, and then realized she must have dropped her doll, because it was no longer in her hand. She turned; there it was facedown on the ground a few meters back, where she'd been lying. When Erzsi gestured at the doll, Lili frowned at her and mouthed, "Hurry up!" and kept going onward. Erzsi scampered back toward the doll, bent over to pick it up, and slipped on some wet leaves. On hands and knees, she pushed herself up and then grabbed the doll. She could still see the group up ahead; they were not far away. Her sister turned and gestured at her and then kept walking. Erzsi brushed herself off, then brushed off the doll. She could easily run and catch up with her family in five seconds. It was then that she noticed that she was not alone. A single wiry, young Russian soldier faced her, legs apart, arms extended like pincers, poised to pounce and grab her. Their eyes met and she thought she saw fear. Maybe because she was just a child, he was not sure how to proceed. She remembered Nadia and her quick fencing techniques. The element of surprise. Just as he lunged for her, she sidestepped, threw Kati at his head, and started to run.

Lili's whispered voice snapped her from her reverie. "Erzsi! What on earth are you doing? Why did you throw your doll?"

"I . . . there was a man . . . a soldier, didn't you see him?"

"Uh, no. I decided to come to fetch you when I saw that you were taking your sweet time. There was nobody else with you," Lili said softly. "Now come on before we lose them!"

"But." Erzsi did not want to accept that she'd imagined the encounter, but there was no other explanation. She was tired and anxious, and her mind was playing tricks on her! She retrieved her doll and followed her sister back to the others. As she ducked under a low tree branch her hat got caught. She stopped and tried to untangle it, but Lili grabbed her hand and yanked. "No time! Leave it!" she said and pulled Erzsi along. They caught up to the others, Erzsi's heart thudding.

A minute later Erzsi noticed lights up ahead, and an icy chill shot down her spine. It was searchlights, for sure. The soldiers were going to arrest them. Or shoot them. Or maybe both. This was it. They'd tried and failed, and here they'd meet their end. She would have sketched this moment if she could have, the woods and the light and the refugees and the sense of imminent doom. She felt her back pocket to make sure the sketch of the demonstration at Petőfi Square was still there. Then she realized that when they detained her, they'd go through her possessions, and the drawing would prove she was not just a refugee, but a rebel, a freedom fighter, a revolutionary. She'd be thrown in prison! A child, maybe, but an example to the rest of Hungary of what happens to rebels, no matter what age! The possibility seemed very real, yet she was not afraid. She would face it bravely. She'd use the time in jail to draw many pictures of places, people, and moments, of her adventures—day after day, pictures and more pictures, memories of what had happened: Mrs. Friedman and her wafers, Sándor the coal man, the ugly tank, the soldiers, the police on the train to Sopron, the border guide with his droopy mustache, the smelly outhouse, the field and the woods, all of it. She'd put them up on the walls of her prison cell and surround herself with the story of these last few weeks.

Just then their guide stopped and turned to face the group. "There, up ahead, that's the border, keep going toward the lights," László said softly. "The woods will end, and you'll reach a road. And you'll be in Austria. Now it's time for me to go back, so good luck to you all! *Auf Wiedersehen!*"

CHAPTER 23
November 28

Austrian soil. Free soil. That's what they were standing on.

Anna fished the little green leather-bound 1956 daily planner and a pen from her handbag and made a notation for November 28: 7:30 p.m.—Free soil.

"Anna, do you have to mark every moment down in that little book?" her husband asked.

"Yes. I do." She tucked the planner and pen back into her bag. "I like to keep a record of what happens."

Anna felt sick and wasn't sure whether the nausea was relief or fear of the unknown, or perhaps a little of both. They didn't have to run anymore, they were safe. The countryside did not look that different from Hungary, not at all. Before they could make any further decisions, Tamás said good-bye. He was going to strike out on his own and see what he could do; he did not want to burden them with his presence any further. Lili tried to dissuade him from leaving but he smiled and said he'd be fine, gave them each a hug, and then headed off to the left, following some of the others they'd crossed over with. The Molnárs were standing there, uncertain what to do next, when an Austrian border guard suddenly materialized, approaching them but taking his time. The guard started speaking German. Luckily Anna was fluent, so she stepped forward.

"Who are you and where do you come from?" he asked gruffly, yet she could see the short young man had a glimmer of sympathy in his blue eyes. His pink cheeks and runny nose made him look like a child and seem less threatening.

"We are the Molnár family from Budapest, and we are seeking asylum from Soviet oppression." She spoke those words as if she'd rehearsed them carefully, but they came from her mouth spontaneously. She was proud of herself for being able to formulate a relatively complex sentence in German. The others with whom they'd crossed the border had veered to the left after reaching Austria probably also to be met by a guard at some point; but some other escapees had now materialized from the woods and were also introducing themselves to this guard.

"All right, then. Come along, follow me." It struck Anna that they were safe now. The Russians, though they were probably only a few hundred meters away, could not touch them! The guard led them silently along the dirt road past a few open fields and to a farm with a crooked old barn, its old gray doors wide open, revealing a dozen or so other Hungarians. "You can sleep here," the guard said. "We've an arrangement with the farmer." He seemed bored with the whole situation, hoping for the day when he could go back to his regular duties, which did not involve leading refugees to barns.

***

After the Molnárs staked out a spot in the far-left corner of the barn, the farmer came and gave them a piece of bread and some milk, and then told them in bare-bones Hungarian that a bus would be coming along in the morning to take them someplace to be processed. They could not stay here for more than one night, because this was meant only for those who'd just crossed over. He closed the barn doors behind him as he left.

Erzsi tried to sleep but the bed was just some hay strewn around the barn floor and the earthy smell with a hint of manure was overpowering. Also, a couple of teenagers kept whispering to each other just loud enough to be disturbing but not clearly enough to be understood.

She finally drifted off late into the night, and when she woke up the barn doors were open again and the barn had emptied out a bit—at least a few of the people had already left. Her parents and sister were already up and chewing on some bread the farmer had given them. Lili handed her sister a piece, and Erzsi stuffed the whole thing in her mouth with one hand while she rubbed her eyes with the other. As she chewed, she reached for her knapsack, but it was gone. Gone!

"Mami! Someone took my knapsack!" Kati and her favorite pair of corduroy pants were gone forever. Stolen! It was probably that whispering couple; they were probably whispering about how they could steal her things. Especially her beloved doll, which had saved her life against the Russian soldier. Though back in the woods she'd convinced herself the soldier had been imaginary, she'd since come to believe that he was in fact real.

"Hmmm, we've been up for a half an hour and we didn't see anything. Someone must have taken it during the night. People are so ugly! We'll get you new things soon," Mrs. Molnár said, hugging her daughter, and Erzsi thought of her hat in the forest too, along with everything else she'd had to leave behind.

For the second time in twelve hours, Erzsi had to use an outhouse, this time waiting on a line of five people to use it. Soon after she finished, the farmer told everyone to wait outside. A few minutes later, a white bus pulled up in front of the barn. The driver got out, stuck two fingers in his mouth and whistled loudly. "*Achtung!*" he said. "*Alle, bitte steigen Sie in den Bus. Ihr geht alle nach Eisenstadt.*" The farmer then translated in his hoarse voice: "Attention. Everyone, please get on the bus. You're all going to Eisenstadt."

The bus ride was almost an hour, but it seemed to take forever. Erzsi sat next to the window and watched the Austrian countryside whiz by. She kept asking her father when they were going to be there, and his answer every time was: "Soon enough, little one." After a while she gave up asking; he had no better idea than she did. Though he'd spent time in Austria long ago, he must have long since forgotten the details of its geography. Her other question: "Why are we going to Eisenstadt?" was met with a shrug and a "We'll see." She knew it must have bothered her father not to be in control of the situation, to be told where to go and what to do. To be a refugee.

When the bus finally came to a stop, the driver popped open the door and told everyone to get out and that they would have to be processed as refugees by the local security director for Burgenland, the province of Austria they were in, and given papers to carry with them for now, until they got a different set of papers.

Erzsi tried to process the scene but there was a lot to take in. They were apparently at a large and bustling refugee camp of some sort. They stood as a group for a few minutes, in front of the bus, and a tall man in a police uniform said in Hungarian that there were some kind Austrians who were willing to take in people for a night or two while other arrangements could be made. A young mother with a one-year-old child on her shoulder raised her hand with a question, but the policeman ignored the woman.

"Listen. I know you may have a lot of questions. There are a lot of you. Not in this particular group I mean, but overall. And we're trying our best to register and process all of you. We must have order." He turned around and gestured at a few people who had been waiting next to their parked cars near the bus. "One at a time," he said. An elegant man in a blue suit addressed the refugees. He said in broken Hungarian that he could take in two people, either separate or together. A young couple at the back of the group waved and pushed their way to the front. They spoke a few hushed words with the elegant man and then headed to his car and drove off.

Next came a heavyset middle-aged man in blue overalls held up by suspenders, who said nothing but held up two fingers. Another couple to Erzsi's left said, "Here!" and the man nodded and gestured for them to follow him. Now a short old woman with a red paisley kerchief over her bright orange-red hair stepped forward, followed by a tall wrinkled old man with a mop of bright white hair on his head. The woman said, "We can take in three people," in flawless Hungarian. Mrs. Molnár waved frantically and said, "Hello! We are three."

The woman said, "Okay. Very good."

The Molnárs stepped forward and then Anna added, ". . . plus one little girl."

The woman frowned. "I'm sorry. Three means three," she said. "We have room for three."

"We're three. She doesn't count; she's just a nothing, a little girl. You'll barely need any extra space for her," Anna said, gesturing dismissively at Erzsi, who hunched over instinctively and tried to look smaller. A nothing! She knew her mother did not mean it, but it still stung.

The old woman seemed amused at this desperation. She looked Erzsi over and then whispered something in the ear of her husband and he nodded and then shrugged. "Okay, yes. Come. I think we can squeeze you all into our car and our apartment."

It was another hour's ride. Mr. Molnár was in the front with the old couple and Mrs. Molnár, Lili, and Erzsi were squished in the back seat. Almost nothing was said the entire ride to Vienna, but once they got into town the Molnárs started to chatter among themselves. The old woman said, "Vienna is a lovely city. I'm sure you'll get to know it in the next few days or weeks or however long you choose to stay. We can only take you for a couple of nights, but we will do our best to make you feel at home and answer any questions you might have about Vienna."

They were shown to a room in the second-floor apartment in a beautiful white stone building on Lowelstrasse, a street lined with nineteenth-century buildings in the heart of Vienna. Erzsi could see why they'd said three people—it was going to be tight. It was a large bedroom, but there was just a king-size bed, a desk and chair, a large dresser, and an armoire.

"This is our bedroom; we'll stay in the spare room so you have enough space. While you're staying here the authorities will be doing your paperwork and finding a place for you at the refugee center in town," the old lady said. "The bathroom is through that door." She pointed to what Erzsi had assumed was just a closet. "We have another bathroom in the hall that we will use, so this one is all yours. Keep it as neat as you found it, and the same goes for the room. Feel free to take showers to refresh yourselves. You may even take a bath, just be sure to use less water than is in the Palatinus." She paused and nodded at their surprise at the reference to Budapest's famous swimming pool, then added: "Full disclosure: I was born in Budapest and met my husband here on a family vacation fifty years ago. My name is Mrs. Krauss, but I was born Erdős. You may call me Erzsébet," she said.

"Hey, that's my name too," Erzsi said, clapping her hands. "No kidding! Well, hello there, other Mrs. Krauss," the woman said with a wry smile that set them all laughing. "Now, since it is still morning and you must be famished, I will throw together some breakfast for you. Come to the dining room in a little while. You'll know when by the smell." She winked and left them alone. Mr. Molnár went to the window and looked down to the street.

"Well, we're in Vienna for better or worse," he said. Erzsi could detect a note of regret in his voice.

"For better, I hope," she said.

"We shall see," he said. "We're really here and I can't believe it." He remained at the window, lost in thought.

Meanwhile, Mrs. Molnár and Lili sat on the bed and remarked how comfortable it felt. Lili flopped down on her back and let out a happy sigh. Erzsi sat down next to her mother and smiled. After spending weeks on mattresses on the floor of their hallway, sitting on a real, properly assembled bed felt incredible.

After a few minutes, Mr. Molnár drew the curtains closed and sat down at the little desk next to the window, and pulled open the drawers one by one, rifling through the contents.

"Jancsi!" Mrs. Molnár said, appalled at the brash invasion of privacy. "Don't do that."

"Aha!" Mr. Molnár said, pulling a small pad of paper and a pen from the middle drawer. "Just what I needed. I'm going to cable Ernő soon and let him know we're in Vienna, but I want to write him a letter also and explain in more detail."

"Can I watch?" asked Erzsi. She sprung up from the bed.

"If you wish. It's about as exciting as watching a kettle of water boil, but sure, why not." He chuckled at his daughter's enthusiasm and began to write.

Dearest Ernő,

I am writing to you from the master bedroom of a lovely old couple's apartment in the heart of old Vienna! I'm sure you've been following the news from a distance, and if the reporting has been accurate in America, which I assume it has, then you understand how dire the situation is in Hungary. We decided to leave Hungary, escaped through the woods near Sopron, and now here we are. I am sending you a cable shortly to let you know we escaped but wanted to write a lengthier letter to explain everything. I wish we could have told you in advance that we were leaving, but I'm sure you understand given the circumstances that was not possible. We arrived in Vienna today and as I briefly mentioned in my cable, I am hoping you can be our sponsor to allow us to come to the United States. Though there are other possible choices, we are thinking that is the best one for us.

There are many details to be worked out, of course, but getting us there is the first step. It will be great to see you again. By the time you read this you may have already written and sent me a letter in reply to my cable but that's okay. There's only so much we can communicate through wiring each other; let's use that only for the essential things as it is rather costly.

We're all tired, mentally and physically, anxious about the future. But it's good knowing you're there in the US. That will make it easier for us because we won't be alone.

As Mr. Molnár was in the midst of his letter the scent of sausages and eggs wafted into the bedroom. Erzsi's stomach was still unsettled from the bus ride, but she was very hungry. Though not usually one to direct the others, she couldn't help herself. "Do you smell that? Come on, guys, let's go, time to eat!"

"Relax yourself, young lady," Mr. Molnár said. "The food will wait for us."

"Well, but Erzsi is right, we should not keep them waiting if they were nice enough to make us breakfast," Mrs. Molnár said gently.

"Fine. I'll finish the letter after. I am actually hungry too. Vienna makes me hungry."

Lili and Erzsi laughed, and Mrs. Molnár looked like she was ready to make a pointed barb but decided to keep it to herself.

✳✳✳

The Krausses set the table with beautiful china that was covered in delicate designs of pale pink and blue flowers. The tablecloth was a royal blue, the silverware was sterling, the red cloth napkins were folded into triangles, and the food was delicious. For a few minutes the Molnárs ate in silence while their hosts looked on, beaming at the ravenous appetites of their guests. It was actually Erzsi who decided it was rude to continue eating without saying a word, so she finished chewing her latest mouthful of scrambled eggs, washed it down with apple juice, and said: "You have such a lovely home."

"Why, thank you, young lady," said Mrs. Krauss. Her husband understood the gist of that compliment and said: "*Vielen danke!*"

"Yes, it's quite lovely," Lili added. "So kind of you to let us stay here."

"Well, you seem to be a perfectly nice family. It's our pleasure. And being Hungarian myself, I am sympathetic to the cause. If it were solely up to my husband here, you might have been out of luck." She laughed, and he smirked at her. "*Ich sage nichts Schlechtes über dich*," she said. "I'm not saying anything bad about you," she repeated in Hungarian for the Molnárs.

"I understand more Hungarian than you think," he said in the Molnárs' native tongue, and everyone laughed. "And I am also more sympathetic to your plight than you might think." He winked.

CHAPTER 24
December 2

So this was Vienna? It was both more and less impressive than Lili had imagined. The buildings were quite attractive and the people looked friendly enough, yet the stores and restaurants could not compete with those of Budapest, in her opinion. For the first time since they left, Lili wondered whether she shouldn't have stayed behind with Ivan. He was a pretty serious boyfriend, after all, and she was old enough to make her own decisions, though her parents had just assumed she was willing to go with them—any other option had never even been offered.

She thought she'd be able to call Ivan right away as soon as she got to Vienna, but her father stopped her, telling her that it was very expensive to make anything except the most important calls, and they had to conserve their money for now. She tried to argue that Ivan was in fact an important call, but after a minute she realized it was over between them. She'd never see him again. What was the point in prolonging the relationship? She had to start over, and so did he. There was no chance he would come to America. Leaving Budapest meant cutting certain ties.

She'd find a new boyfriend and new friends there. That was the only way to make a new life.

She was eighteen and she knew that she'd have to get a job quickly and help support the family. What kind of work could she do? She'd been in technical training in Budapest, but that was cut short by their departure. Without good knowledge of English, she feared she'd have a hard time finding work. And also, she'd probably be stuck sharing a room with her little sister for the indefinite future. Erzsi was okay, but she could be pretty annoying and immature. But it'd be all right in the end.

None of these hardships were permanent. The upsetting end to the revolution, the harrowing escape, the stay in Vienna—they were all just part of a road that would lead to stability and happiness. At least that is what Mami had told her the other day.

Lili closed her eyes for a moment and tried to conjure up the sound of Ivan's accordion but she couldn't. Try as she might, she could not. She could barely even picture his face. How could it be that easy to forget? She sighed.

Mami and Erzsi had gone out, strolling around town and window-shopping. They'd asked whether she wanted to accompany them, but lately she felt like a third wheel. And Apu had gone in search of an old business associate who supposedly had a shop in Vienna. Lili was alone and preferred to spend the time in their room at the Krauss house. She could hear them downstairs, talking in lively German.

Lili heard the front door shut and went to the window. She saw the Krausses walking slowly, arm in arm, down the busy street. They soon blended in with everyone else: businessmen, mothers pushing strollers, old men hobbling along with canes, children playing in the street—it could have been a scene on Andrássy Street, or any street anywhere, really. But it felt very different from the Budapest Lili knew. The Viennese had no cares, their freedom was not compromised, their lives were not in jeopardy. There were no soldiers watching them, and no food shortages or tanks in the streets. She thought again of Ivan, and of her grandma and cousins and aunts and uncles. Hopefully they were all okay. Hopefully they'd made the right decision in staying behind, the right decision for them. "Leaving was the right decision for us," she said aloud, though the words sounded hollow when she spoke them, so she repeated them with more conviction: "Leaving was the right decision for us!" Satisfied, she made her way to the bed and curled up for a nice afternoon nap, determined to enjoy the quiet before everyone got home.

CHAPTER 25
December 4

Erzsi walked along Hauptstrasse with her new friend Viki, down the slight hill and around a bend, to the candy store a few blocks away. Viki was an inch taller and a year older, and she alternated between one of three red and green plaid skirts accompanied by stiff high-heeled black leather shoes that looked uncomfortable. She had arrived at the refugee center a week and a half before the Molnárs, and her parents, preoccupied with tending to Viki's three-year-old brother, let her explore the Landstrasse district without restriction. Viki had wandered around most of the immediate area by herself and knew where every child-friendly shop was located within a five-kilometer radius. At first, she regaled her new friend with stories of some of the boutiques and stores, and then Erzsi asked whether she could come along. This was their second trip to the candy store together and Erzsi was eager to take a walk and distract herself from the uncertainty of her current existence.

When she and Viki first saw each other in the refugee center and realized that they were the same age, that was enough to draw them to each other. After exchanging their escape stories (Viki's was more harrowing; her family's guide had abandoned them halfway to the border and left them to find their own way to Austria, which they barely did), they spent time playing or exploring the neighborhood. And what a beautiful neighborhood it was! The Hauptstrasse was lined with beautiful old three- and four-story buildings. It reminded her of Budapest, but it was fresher, brighter, and cheerier. The Hauptstrasse itself seemed like a candy store, lined with visual treats every step of the way. Erzsi found herself wiping a tear from her eye as she walked, overwhelmed by this familiar yet foreign place.

"Hey there, what's the matter?" Viki asked.

"I dunno," Erzsi said. "Feeling a little emotional. Sad, I guess, is the word. Vienna is great. But I'm homesick. I miss Budapest already. I think Vienna makes me miss it more. Doesn't it remind you of Budapest?"

"No. Not really," Viki said with a shrug.

"Like, we're here by the grace of God, we made it safely and all. But still . . ." Erzsi's voice trailed off.

Viki smirked. "The grace of what? Psshhh." She waved her hand in the air as if shooing a fly. "There is no God." She was silent for a moment then asked cheerily, "So what kind of candy do you want to get?"

But Erzsi could not leave such a statement out there. Though religion was not a major part of her life, her friend's words felt like a slap in the face. "What do you mean there is no God? Of course, there is."

"Well," she said, squeezing Erzsi's arm. "You can believe what you want. I am pretty sure there is none. My mom and dad think so also. We're atheists, all of us." Viki had taken some coins from her pocket and was counting them out. "Still getting used to this Austrian money, but I think I should have enough for a nice treat! Maybe one of those dark chocolate squares! Look, the coins are made of aluminum just like Hungarian coins. Most places they aren't like this. My grandfather has traveled a lot and he brought me back money from France, Germany, and England. The money is much heavier."

As much as the thought of an imminent candy purchase was exciting, and the observations on coin composition were interesting, Erzsi was fixated on her friend's admission. "So, you don't think that we should thank any higher power for getting us to Austria safely? And getting you here also? It was just luck?"

"Let's see here. Your guide followed through and got you across, so that was not a higher power; it was your guide knowing the way. As for us, our guide abandoned us and left us to fend for ourselves. Maybe it was just luck for us or maybe it was my dad's instincts. If he didn't follow his instincts, or was careless, we'd not have made it across. Why would a higher power let one of us go smoothly and let the other nearly get captured or shot?"

"But that's exactly the argument for a God. He did get you across. Your guide abandoned you and God helped your father get you across."

"God would not have allowed our guide to abandon us!

Don't you see?" She narrowed her eyes and stared at her friend's face. "No, you don't see. But anyway, if there's a higher power then why is he destroying the country we love? Why didn't he let the freedom fighters win? Why is he forcing us to escape? You can look at it that way, can't you?" An elderly couple shuffled by slowly, arm in arm, and the old man tipped his green-feathered fedora at the two girls. They smiled and waved. Viki continued. "So maybe you will look at that cute old couple and say, 'Look how God blessed them with a long and happy marriage.' I would also say look over at that guy." She pointed to a bench with a bearded, disheveled middle-aged man feeding some pigeons from a paper bag filled with crumbs. "Is he blessed too?"

"Well, I suppose he is. Who's to say he's not happy?" Erzsi felt her pulse quickening. Viki's newly admitted religious views were maddening. Erzsi grabbed her friend's hand and pulled her across the street toward the man.

"Excuse me, are you happy?" she shouted at him when they were within range.

He replied something in German with a shrug and Viki laughed. "He doesn't speak Hungarian, silly. But I do speak a little German." She let go of Erzsi's hand and approached the man. "*Sind Sie glücklich?*"

He squinted, making his small eyes disappear within a sea of wrinkles, stopped tossing bread crumbs, and tilted his head like one of the birds he was feeding. For some reason, his gaze settled on Erzsi and not Viki. "*Ich bin weder glücklich noch unglücklich,*" he said, then lowered his eyes and continued to feed the pigeons, who were flapping excitedly at the prospect of more food.

"He's not happy, he's not unhappy," Viki said as they crossed back over to the other side of the street, on which the candy shop was visible in the distance. "He just is."

"And what does that prove?" asked Erzsi.

"Exactly. What does it prove?"

"You're an odd one," Erzsi told her friend. Now she was ready to change the topic back to candy, but it was too late; she'd opened the door and Viki was ready to explore the subject more thoroughly.

Viki pursed her lips and then tapped them with a finger. "Maybe that old couple who just passed us hate each other. Maybe they love each other. Or maybe it's something in between. Who knows?"

"Then go ask them!" Erzsi said, laughing.

"Very well, I will." And she ran after the couple, to Erzsi's horror. So persistent, that one.

"*Verzeihung, sag mir, ob ihr glücklich seid?*" she shouted.

The old man bent over and said something softly and whatever it was it sent Viki skipping back toward her friend, a goofy smile on her face.

"So they're happy, I was right?" Erzsi asked.

"Not exactly. The old guy scowled and said to leave them alone or he would call the police on me. So, you see my point?"

"Not really," Erzsi lied. She did see a point but it was an ugly one. There was a God but the whole Garden of Eden situation happened, so what did Viki expect? Puppies and roses to rain from the sky nonstop? Grace and blessings still happened, everywhere, every day.

"The point is, there is no logic to anything. That man is not happy, he's not anything. He just exists. Shouldn't he be happy? Shouldn't we all be happy? In our own country instead of here, or some other country?"

"But you forgot the story of Adam and Eve and the apple. Adam ate it. That was the end of paradise. You can't expect everything to be perfect. Not everything. But that does not mean there's no God."

"So, because someone thousands of years ago ate an apple, we are all suffering, or some of us are and others aren't? Paradise lost because of that, but God still loves us. Hmm. If I eat a banana now, will that cause some effects that will last thousands of years? Sounds a little strange to me."

"You don't go to church?"

"Why would I go to church? I told you I am an atheist."

Erzsi looked at a tall white steeple on the next block. She remembered the towering Gothic steeple of the centuries-old Matthias Church in Budapest. Church steeples always made Erzsi pause in silence for a moment. They apparently did not have that effect on Viki, who was now babbling on about what kind of candy to buy. She said the word "*lakritze*" several times, as if she was practicing the pronunciation.

"What are you doing?" Erzsi asked.

"I am saying 'licorice.' I looked it up in the dictionary before we left. It's not on the shelf, it's behind the counter in a jar. Gotta know how to ask for it!"

They'd arrived at the candy store. Erzsi held the door for her friend and they went inside. Erzsi grabbed a couple of chocolate bars while Viki went to the clerk and said, "*Lakritze, bitte.*" The clerk shook his head. "*Wir haben keine mehr.*"

Erzsi did not understand the words but she knew he said, "No more licorice!" She smiled.

"Don't worry. There's plenty of licorice in America." She laughed and thought, *And plenty of churches too.*

"We're not going to America," Viki said, picking up a couple of chocolate bars herself.

"What do you mean?"

"My father says Australia is better. Many Hungarians are going there; at least, that's what he says. And I believe him, because why would he lie about that?"

"Are you saying atheists don't lie?"

"This has nothing to do with atheism. Not everyone wants to go to America. Personally, I don't care either way. I don't know anyone in either place so what's the difference?"

"Well, I do," she lied. "My dear uncle Ernő. And I miss him and can't wait to hug him again."

"Good for you, Erzsi." They paid for their candy and left the store. Viki immediately unwrapped a candy bar and started to eat it. She got chocolate on her face, but Erzsi decided not to tell her.

CHAPTER 26
December 12

János Molnár looked at the oversized sheet of paper that was filled with detailed instructions. This is what their lives had come down to right now—forms, paperwork, legal documents of all kinds, numbers and codes and official stamps. At the top left of this particular form, his name was written in a rather bright blue ink. Where it said, "Name of head of family," an Austrian official had written: Molnár, János; the last name in overly large, sloppy all-capital letters and the first name in a messy script. He squinted. It looked like "Jmenor" instead of János. Stupid bureaucrats. But could he blame them? Were they thrilled with the sudden influx of Hungarians into their country? It was a nightmare to have to process them. The form was in Hungarian and English, with not a single word in German—clearly devised for the many thousands of refugees who fled from Hungary into Austria with the intention of ending up in America. For many families, Austria was just a stopping point along the way.

Total number of persons in family: 4. The way it was written the number almost looked like a nine. Imagine a family of nine having to flee across the border! It would be quite challenging. Four was hard enough.

Section 1 of the form, which said, "Please GO NOW with the other members of your family (if any) to the photographer, in Room No. 5 downstairs, and show him this form" had been crossed out with a wavy blue line. János would have preferred to go to Room 5 and take care of this immediately, but that was not an option.

Instead, he was to follow the instructions in Section 2, which said, "On December 13, 1956"—the date had been filled in again in that awful blue color—"at 14:30–15:30 take this paper, and your AUSTRIAN POLICE IDENTITY CARDS to Schmidgasse 14. Take all members of your family with you (by members of a family we mean ONLY your spouse and/or unmarried children under 21 years of age). DO NOT attempt to report at any other date or time as you will be admitted at Schmidgasse 14 only on this date. ALSO, you will not be admitted there unless you have this form AND your Austrian identity certificate." He reread this several times to make sure he'd properly absorbed all the dos and don'ts. When he was satisfied that he understood the directions, he reached into his pocket and pulled out the Austrian identity certificate. "Federal Police Headquarters" it said menacingly at the top. It seemed to be in order. Good. The paper was valid until January 2, 1957. They had to be out of the country by then. A date that was less than three weeks away.

A note at the bottom of the paper read "IMPORTANT: If you miss your appointment at Schmidgasse 14, or lose this paper, we will have to delay your case indefinitely, and you may even miss going to the United States entirely."

Those last words sent a cold shiver through his chest. Indefinitely and entirely, what a pair of words! Miss it entirely! And then what? How strange to think that after all their efforts to escape—running through the woods with almost no possessions to their name, risking everything for a better life, for freedom—their hopes could be dashed if they missed a single appointment.

He put the paper aside and studied the map of Vienna. He traced the path with his finger—Schmidgasse 14 was not that far but it was not that close either. Twenty minutes by foot. Maybe more. There was probably a bus or tram that could get them there, but being a stranger to this city, he'd not attempt to navigate the transit system. This was not a vacation after all. At least by foot there would be no mistakes.

Beyond this form and the photograph, their ability to enter America also rested on his brother sponsoring them, but that seemed to be a done deal—so far, Ernő had been very helpful and willing to get them safely to the US.

He pulled Ernő's last letter, dated December 5, from his pocket and reread the opening paragraph. It was a good thing he'd typed the letter, because his handwriting had always been terribly illegible.

You may already know that I am not the best correspon-
dent and I can't really describe my feelings very well, but
when we found out that you were in Vienna, Maria and I

were overjoyed to the point of tears. It is only a matter of days, at most weeks, that we will all be here in the United States, together. There is so much more to say, but I won't waste time or paper trying to pour out my thoughts. We will have years to come for that once you are here, near to me. You can be sure that we will both suffocate you with as much love and warmth as we have, and we will do our best to help you get used to life here quickly and easily.

I will try to gather myself and write essential things. I think you've been moving forward since arriving in Vienna. If it turns out that there are difficulties, the head of JDC, Miss Flora Levine, who is a very good friend of our family, and another good friend, Sidney Gerber, have worked together in Europe on similar post-war migrations.

What led you to settle in Vienna? I know you worked there many years ago, and I know it would be a lot easier if you could stay in your profession for a similar audience, with perfect knowledge of language, but I'm only going to understand it if there's something special in Austria. Because the future is HERE in America. It is everywhere here, all around.

Jancsi refolded the letter and smiled. For years he'd seen his younger brother as a restless soul in search of himself, trying to find a better life. Back in '39 when Ernő left Hungary, he was the upstart, the rebel making a rash decision to leave, though, yes, Jancsi did give him a little money to help him along. Then came the war and suddenly this rash decision seemed brilliant. He'd left just in time. Ernő wound up enlisting in the American army and helping to liberate Europe from the Nazis. Now, really for the first time, he saw his younger brother as an equal. Now it was Jancsi who was trying to find a better life and needed a brother's help. Now it was his little brother who was the beacon for the future.

Not that Vienna wasn't lovely. It was a beautiful city, comparable in size, culture, and history to Budapest. And quite a nice address to boast, at that. He could easily picture himself handing out business cards with an address featuring some long-winded German street name, and saying to potential customers, "My shop is in downtown Vienna. Stop by next time you're in town!" He scratched his chin and nodded slowly. If they stayed in Austria, they'd have to find lodgings in some little Viennese outskirt until they could afford to move in to a good neighborhood in the city proper. That could take a couple of years, just as opening his own store would. He might even have to start off working in someone else's shop first, an abhorrent thought. But that didn't mean he would neglect a daily cup of coffee in one of the luxurious cafés—no, that would be an essential part of becoming Austrian.

A car horn beeped outside and snapped Jancsi out of his Viennese reverie. Staying here had never been the plan, nor did he think the Austrians were taking very many refugees permanently. And actually, being so close to his old home would be a bit torturous, and perhaps tempting. It would be like breaking up with a beloved girlfriend but still being able to see her house in the distance every day.

No, to escape, he would have to get as far away as possible, not be within a couple of hours' train ride of the border. A fresh start, unfortunately, meant wiping Hungary away, leaving it across an ocean and making a clean break, maybe even leaving the coat business entirely. America was going to be his reinvention, his rebirth. János Molnár, brain surgeon? Well, maybe not that drastic, but one never knew.

Funny though, with all these thousands of refugees heading for the US, and for New York more specifically, how many old friends, distant cousins, and acquaintances might he encounter once there? Perhaps the jolly old widowed neighbor who lived across the courtyard, the redheaded pharmacist at the drugstore downtown, his retired former accountant—anything was possible. Jancsi had already run into several former Budapest residents in the last couple of weeks—including an old friend from grade school whom he'd not seen in thirty years. Maybe New York might hold more familiar faces. The mystery and promise of that thought propelled him, and he stood up suddenly, heart racing. December 13 was tomorrow, and though the appointment was in the afternoon, he'd be sure to get them all up at the first rays of sunlight so they'd be ready with their papers to get photographed and be one step closer to Ernő, to America, and to their new life.

CHAPTER 27
December 19

Vienna seemed especially gray and cold to Erzsi on this December day, both in temperature and in general atmosphere. The entire population of the city seemed to be on the streets today, but the throng of people had no cheer. All of them were in a determined rush, bustling about with a single-minded focus on their last-minute holiday preparations, multiple shopping bags in hand as they chattered excitedly to each other in unintelligible German. A couple of young men brushed past Mrs. Molnár, one of them almost knocking her over before offering a quick "Oh, sorry!" over his shoulder. The Viennese had purpose, which made Erzsi feel even more like a drifter, an extra in a movie about someone else's reality. Even the tourists, who were easy to spot because of their slower pace, occasional photograph taking, and general gawking and pointing, seemed to fit in somehow. For a couple of minutes, a few flakes of snow started to fall, big wet ones that fluttered by slowly and disappeared when they hit the ground. Erzsi caught one on her palm and watched it melt.

They walked past a newspaper stand, and a headline caught her eye.

"Hey, come on, don't stop suddenly or we'll get separated and you'll be lost."

Erzsi tugged on her mother's coat sleeve and pointed to the newspaper stand. "No, look, Mami, look!"

"What? What am I looking at? What's the matter?"

"The newspaper. The headline . . ."

They approached the newsstand but Mrs. Molnár was still puzzled. Erzsi grabbed a copy of a Viennese newspaper and held it up. On the front page was a large photograph of Nadia Andor holding her fencing foil. Mrs. Molnár said, "Ohh!" gave the vendor a coin and started to read the article out loud, translating it from German to Hungarian as she went. "United States to Admit 35 Hungarian Olympians Who Want to Defect."

United States Attorney General Brownell today authorized the admission of 35 Hungarian Olympians, four Romanians, and one Czech athlete who were seeking political asylum. All have expressed their dissatisfaction with the Communist regimes in their homelands and their unwillingness to return.

According to Brownell: "These aliens will be permitted to enter the United States temporarily and ultimately apply for permanent resident status, if Congress enacts legislation making it possible for them to become permanent residents of the United States."

A similar action was taken by the government earlier this autumn to allow 15,000 Hungarian refugees, who fled to Austria to escape the Soviet regime, into the country.

When the Olympics ended this month, 45 of the 175 Hungarian athletes decided not to fly back to Hungary. Of those 45, some decided to stay in Australia or go to other countries. Among those who stayed behind are László Tábori, a sprinter, his coach Mihály Iglói, and women's fencer Nadia Andor. Some of those who are defecting have family members who fled Hungary in the last few weeks just before or during the Olympic games and are now making plans to meet up with their loved ones.

Erzsi clapped her hands. "Maybe we will be reunited in America," she said. "I hope we can reach her somewhere."

"Perhaps," Mrs. Molnár said. "When things settle down, we can try to call her mother and see what she knows."

"Maybe Aunt Regina has escaped too!" Erzsi said.

"Knowing her, I doubt it. She is anxious enough just getting on the subway to go shopping, never mind trying to run through the woods while being shot at."

"Maybe. Though these days people do things they'd not normally do."

A woman carrying a bundle of six shirt boxes tied together with string bumped into Erzsi and apologized profusely. "Sorry, sorry!"

"It's okay." Mrs. Molnár shook her head. "Whenever we get out of Vienna won't be soon enough for me," she told her daughter.

"Apa will be so happy to read this article," Erzsi said. "He will be happy that we can see Nadia again."

"Well, maybe. America is big, though, so don't get too

excited yet. But I am glad to hear that at least one of your cousins made the same decision we did. I am starting to think this is actually the right thing, what we chose to do. It's for the best."

CHAPTER 28
December 23

János Molnár reread the letter from his sister-in-law, Maria, in America, dated December 17. It had already been passed around and absorbed by the other three family members. It was nice to read Hungarian again after being surrounded by the German language everywhere in Vienna.

I can't tell you how much we anticipate your arrival. Our president has promised that everyone will be here by the end of this year. It would be great if we could all be together at Christmas, though it is rapidly approaching.

I don't even know Lili and Erzsi; Lili had only just been born when we came to the United States. Oh, they will love it very much here. It is easy to acclimate at their age. And besides, from what I have heard, schools hardly give European refugee children any homework. Here, the teachers cannot be Caesars, because it's the children who are the kings. It is also a fact that there are not so many nasty, rude kids anywhere else as there are in the United States, but at least they are all happy to be treated so well.

Jancsi, as far as you are concerned, you can certainly

work yourself up to a respectable position here, if not as high as perhaps you could in Vienna. I also think it would be more favorable for you to be here and sleep peacefully, rather than so close to the Russians. That actor you like so much, László Bekefy, once said that many Jewish families would have been saved during the war, because they did have a chance to come out of Hungary, they just didn't want to leave their assets behind. Bekefy called it a sideboard complex, after the place where so many people keep their valuables hidden. So János, don't have a sideboard complex.

Mr. Molnár sighed. It was too late for a sideboard complex; he'd already left almost everything behind anyway. Sure, the family would salvage what they could, but who knew when or if he'd get it back. There was no going back now, no return across the border—that would result in certain punishment. Yes, it was true, he'd be far away from the Russians in America, but that alone did not ensure a peaceful sleep. Not at all. He would sleep, yes. But how would it be possible to rest in the same way he used to on Andrássy Street for the last twenty years?

Anna said there was no need for the money I sent. Money is important, but not the most important thing. Keep it there, use it. Write if you need something, and certainly let us know if you leave. If you see good clothing, buy something for yourself; it can't be more expensive in Vienna than here.

Anna may have been too proud to admit needing money, but it was definitely needed. At this point, pride was useless and foolish. Leaving Hungary, they instantly went from comfortable to in need of comforting. So, they'd use Maria's money for whatever essentials they required, and he'd not be afraid to ask for more. He would pay Ernő and Maria back as soon as he could.

✳ ✳ ✳

It was almost Christmas and Vienna was decked out in festive joy. The scent of pine needles permeated the crisp air and twinkling lights adorned some of the storefronts and residences. Everywhere you looked, there were wreaths hung on doors and Christmas trees sold by street vendors. But Erzsi was not feeling festive, she was missing Budapest more than ever. Seeing family was a big part of their holiday traditions, all of which would have to be put aside this year. How long had they been in Austria now? How many days? Would they ever be allowed to go to the United States?

"Come, stop moping around. I know what will cheer you up," Mrs. Molnár said. "We will call your aunt in Budapest to wish her a Merry Christmas!"

The voice that answered was familiar, but it was not Julia. It was Anna's niece Zsuzsa.

"Oh, Anna! So good to hear your voice!" she said. They'd talked before, weeks ago when the Molnárs had first escaped, but it was nice to talk to her again, especially so close to Christmas.

"Yours too. And I hate to admit it, but I am sorry actu-ally—I think I dialed the wrong number. I meant to call your aunt Julia and I must have dialed your number by accident."

"No, this is the right number. I am here in her apart-ment rescuing some things. Julia is in Vienna also! She escaped two days ago! She's staying at the Hotel Regina with Pali. Go and find her!"

Anna could hardly believe it! She blurted the news to the rest of the family, and all they donned their coats and hurried on foot to the Hotel Regina. As soon as they burst into the lobby, they saw Pali sitting on a chair watching a football match on television. He applauded as one team scored a goal.

"Hello, cousin," Erzsi said with a disguised deeper voice. When he didn't react, she added. "Ahem. Cousin Pali, that is. Hello, Cousin Pali from Budapest, Hungary!"

He turned around and his eyes lit up. He pulled a purple lollipop from his mouth and Erzsi could smell the grape. Oh, how much she would love her own lollipop right now! Pali licked his lips and said: "Will you look at this. If it isn't my old partner in crime and one of the original freedom fighters." He smirked and Erzsi hurried over to give him a hug.

"We're just a couple of revolutionaries, aren't we?" she said.

"That's us, in the flesh!" He gave her a playful elbow to the ribs and she rolled her eyes. "On the run from the authorities, because we are dangerous!" He laughed heartily and Erzsi kissed his cheek, which made him turn bright red.

"Hello there, young man. What a surprise this is," said Mr. Molnár, tipping his hat at his nephew.

"Hello, Auntie and Uncle! Hello, Lili! Good to see you all!"

They explained how they found him and he led them to the room where he and his mother were staying. He knocked sharply and Julia called from within, "It's open, silly."

He pushed the door open. Erzsi's aunt was sitting on the edge of the four-post queen-size bed, reading through a brochure about the hotel. "Did you know this hotel was built in the..." Her voice trailed off when she looked up and saw the Molnárs standing next to her son. "Oh my goodness, Anna!" she exclaimed, clapped her hands, and carried her tall, delicate frame over to the doorway. "Please come in!"

"It's only luck that we found Zsuzsa in your apartment when we called over there. Or else we might not have ever known you were in Vienna!" This was the happiest Erzsi had seen her mother in weeks; she was beaming at the sight of her older sister. "Now tell us how on earth you managed to wind up here in one of Vienna's most exclusive hotels!"

"It was very coincidental. We ran into an old friend of the family while we were making a telephone call to Budapest from an Austrian town near the border, and this fellow had his car so he drove us to Vienna, to this hotel where he was just about to check out. He checked out and we checked into the same room. We only had enough for a one night's stay but a few phone calls later I was in touch with a rich philanthropist whom I once helped long ago. He gave us enough money to stay here for a few weeks!"

"Random encounter? Rich philanthropist? What luck," said Mr. Molnár. Erzsi could always detect when her father was jealous, and it happened often with his sister-in-law for some reason.

"Luck, yes, for now. But we don't have a sponsor to go to the United States as you do. So that'll be our challenge."

"Oh, I hope you can find someone soon," Mrs. Molnár said to her sister.

"I'm making a list of potential people to contact."

"I wish we could be of more help, but it looks like we will be leaving within the week," said Mr. Molnár. "In the meantime, we can get you some new clothes, so you don't look like refugees." It was true, their clothes were dirty, and Pali's shirt was ripped in a couple of places.

"That would be appreciated. We got a little messy crossing the border."

"There is some charity that is providing clothing for people like us. We will give you the information," said Mrs. Molnár. She smiled and added, "Oh, Julia, it's so good to see you! We can spend Christmas together at least!"

"Yes, we can, and you will all come here. We have a little extra money for a nice meal. We'll celebrate!"

Erzsi and Lili were already celebrating by jumping onto the big luxurious bed and sighing contently as they rolled around. Pali laughed and joined his cousins as the adults watched, smiling with joy at this reunion.

CHAPTER 29
December 31

The startlingly bright red rose.

This is what Erzsi focused on, not the hulking silver airplane onto which it was painted, not the unintelligible English words "Military Air Transport Service" that were printed on the plane in all capital letters, nor the fact that they were about to leave Europe for the first time and probably forever. The rose was something, at least. It was a symbol of life and hope. It was color on an otherwise dull military transport plane. Ahh, if old Péter Szüle were alive to see this; he'd have realized that a little color is a good thing, that drab and mysterious art is not so great. Rembrandt schmembrandt. Marta needed a red rose in her hair. Imagine that! How the painting would have been improved, livened, by just that one touch. Maybe Szüle was not in a mindset where he could have conceived of such things. Maybe he had no roses in him to give his models—real or imaginary. She thought of what Kálmán had told her and realized that maybe Szüle just didn't want the viewer to see a rose and think rosy thoughts. Erzsi decided that when she finally did paint that scene with the tank, she would drop a rose onto it—or maybe a poppy instead. The flower in her painting would represent blood while this rose represented love, the love that the United States apparently had for Hungarians. She smiled and then found herself being tugged along by her father.

"Come, come, stop daydreaming, it's time to board the plane!" he said.

"Sorry, Papa," she replied. It seemed like months ago that they'd celebrated Christmas with Aunt Julia and Cousin Pali, back in Vienna. Things were happening fast. Once they had the clearance to go to the United States, that was that. They were on their way.

The family walked slowly, filing in a line of other tired refugees, maybe fifty in total, toward the metal stairs that had been rolled into place beneath the cabin door. Erzsi's shoes clanked on the steps as she climbed up. She was suddenly afraid of the height, of being how many meters above the tarmac? Seven? Ten? Twenty? A chill shot through her as she realized this was nothing; the plane would be thousands of meters in the air, not a mere ten or twenty above the ground. Once again, her father's voice imploring her to pick up the pace brought her back to the reality of the moment. They were now inside this dark vehicle and it smelled nothing like the train they'd ridden to Munich on; it smelled of leather boots and musty attics and burlap sacks.

They were all led to their seats and told to strap their safety belts on. A few basic things were explained, like the location of the toilets, when they'd be fed, and some safety measures. Mr. Molnár asked Erzsi whether she wanted to be next to the window, and after hesitating she said yes. Curiosity won out over fear. This could be (hopefully!) her only airplane flight ever, so why not make the most of it?

Lili and her mother were busy chatting nervously about buying new clothes in America as other passengers filed into the plane. Like the Molnárs, they had very little in the way of belongings. It was some comfort to hear all the chattering in Hungarian, to know these fellow travelers were all on the same mission. They were probably from all corners of the country—she could detect variations in their accents that said they were definitely not from the big city—but they were Hungarians nonetheless. There was a tall blond girl of similar age sitting nearby. She gave Erzsi a friendly nod, but Erzsi quickly averted her eyes. She was not in a talkative mood, not now. The thought of new American clothes was not comforting. Erzsi liked her old clothes, though she recognized she could not survive indefinitely with just the few things from Budapest and the few more acquired in Vienna. And though she'd never given much thought to her father's coats before, now she wished she had two armfuls of coats to bring with her, to wrap herself in, to shield herself from the elements and New York in general.

Suddenly the plane roared to life, the propellers started to whir. She braced for movement but nothing came, not for several minutes, until finally the plane jerked to motion and started to roll slowly. It moved at this leisurely pace for a while, going straight first then turning once and turning again. Erzsi wondered if the plane was ever going to leave the ground and at that moment it came to a complete halt. A few seconds later another similar-looking airplane (without a red rose) roared into the air in the distance. Erzsi watched its ascent and swallowed hard.

"What's going on, Papa, when are we leaving?" she asked.

"I have no idea. I have never flown in a plane either." He paused. "Though I would guess that we were waiting for that other plane to leave first." As the rest of the passengers came to this realization too, that departure was imminent, the chattering faded to a few hushed whispers.

"May I hold your hand?"

"Yes, sure," he said without offering it. She reached over and grabbed his left hand and squeezed. Now the plane began a mad straight dash, picking up speed. She got dizzy watching the scenery go by outside. Then the plane lifted off the ground and the fact that she could feel it so much startled her. The machine was much more unsteady than she'd imagined it would be. It wobbled and veered to the right and then to the left as it climbed at a rate that seemed unsafe. The ground below receded at a dizzying pace, the runway and the surrounding countryside shrinking away with every passing second.

"We're lucky," Mr. Molnár said, nodding.

Erzsi waited for him to explain but he closed his eyes in silence. The plane rose suddenly and Erzsi's stomach rose with it. She gulped. "What do you mean?"

"Your uncle, when he went to America, he had to take a boat."

"You mean he's lucky?" she said as the plane hit a pocket of turbulence and shook.

"No. We're the lucky ones. The boat trip took days. This is just hours."

"I would not mind that, I think." The fresh sea air, the sunshine, maybe a dolphin here and there; an ocean voyage would have been like a vacation.

"Your aunt was sick the whole time from the big waves. Bad weather followed them the entire way. This is much better, trust me." His words did not match his tone, which was not convincing.

She wanted to reply but she was busy watching the thick fluffy white clouds they were rumbling through. *I'm in the clouds*, she told herself. *That's pretty special.*

"They told me when we boarded that the flight would take about fourteen hours," Mr. Molnár said, as if it were some kind of astonishing engineering feat that would please his daughter. To Erzsi, fourteen hours in this unsteady contraption was inconceivable, especially since barely twenty minutes had elapsed since they took off. "Have a nap or something," Mr. Molnár said, extricating his hand from hers and then patting it gently as if it were the head of a dog sitting by his side. Sleeping would be nice, but Mami and Lili were chattering again, and the plane was wobbling and bumping, and it felt like that horrible bus ride into the countryside on a dirt road two summers ago, only worse because they could not beg the pilot to stop so they could get out and regain their balance for a few minutes. Erzsi knew she'd never sleep. But she closed her eyes anyway and clenched her fists so tightly that her fingernails dug into her palms. Eventually she felt herself drift off.

* * *

When Erzsi woke up her head was foggy and her stomach hurt. She blinked several times and rubbed her eyes until they were sore. A few voices could be heard toward the back of the cabin, but it was mostly silent. Her parents and Lili were asleep or at least resting. Out the window, she could see nothing but a sheet of clouds below. They were high, high up now, and thankfully, the plane seemed to be more stable. But that was relative—it still wobbled here and there and rose and fell on occasion. From her father's watch she could see they'd now been flying for four hours. Ten more to go!? She took a deep breath. Ten hours was longer than a school day by several hours, longer than a night of sleep, longer than pretty much any single thing she had done or event she had endured.

They were probably over the Atlantic Ocean now. Or were they? The only thing visible out the window was a carpet of clouds some distance below the plane. She tried to picture a map of the world, do some quick math in her head. Maybe not! Maybe they were still over Europe, over England perhaps. In any case this was it, they were really leaving home behind. A tear rolled slowly down her cheek and she let it roll down her neck and disappear. She felt its path quickly dry, imagining a searing sensation and hoping that the tear's path would be visible to everyone, like a tattoo or a branding. She never wanted to wash her face again. She would bear this sorrow forever, a salty trail on her face that would tell people she'd gone through something heart-wrenching. She wanted to cry more but nothing came, and that made her even more melancholy.

There was so much she was losing! Her cousins and aunts and uncles, her loved and hated school, her wide tree-lined boulevard, her stately apartment building, the lush park with its pure white swans, the wafer shop in the courtyard, the elegant cafés and their tempting pastries, the puppet theater—these places suddenly disappeared from her reality. Only traces were left behind in her day-dreams and memories. Her home instantly transformed from a place she knew into place she had once known. Her future was filled with unknown places, yet she could pic-ture them—narrow treeless streets bustling with hurried people, a school with teachers and students who did not speak a word of Hungarian, cafés with strange names that served unfamiliar things, barren parks without an animal in sight, apartment buildings that were twenty stories high and modern and ugly.

The past was wonderful and gone, the future was unknown and daunting—and the present, this fourteen-hour journey into the clouds, was nerve-racking and boring at the same time. She stared at her father's silver watch as the second hand jerked forward slowly. She waited while it made one complete revolution around the face of the watch. Tick. Tick. Tick. Finally (finally!) the hand arrived back at twelve.

So slow, and that was just one measly minute out of sixty minutes in one hour out of ten hours before they arrived in America! That second hand would have to circle the watch another 599 times before the wheels hit the ground in their new home. She thought about just counting those revolutions as a way to preoccupy herself, but she realized that would be worse than just letting the time go by. "A watched pot never boils," as her mother told her many times.

Sitting there wringing her hands, it struck Erzsi that she had no idea what the plan was. Was there even a plan? Her father always spoke of plans. He was a man with a plan; no matter how small the occasion, he had a plan for it. For breakfast, there had to be a plan—"Tomorrow we will have scrambled eggs and fresh rolls from the bakery." For a walk in the park, there had to be a plan—"We will take the path on the left and circle around twice, then go by the pond." So for something as important as America, there must be some grand plan that she was simply not privy to. "You're too young to worry about these things," as her sister liked to tell her. But she was a worrier and had been one since she could remember. And anyway, she was not that young anymore. Almost eleven! Practically a teenager! It was easy for Lili to imagine her sister's serene childhood indifference, but Erzsi felt there was no such thing. The cogs and gears in her mind were always turning, like an over-wound watch, and that inevitably led to nervous somersaults within her stomach.

They would land . . . where? And then what? Uncle Ernő would eventually come get them, that much she knew.

But beyond that, the future was like Marta's painting—unknowable and hidden from view. She wanted to ask all the questions right then, but she did not want to know the answers. She was afraid that her parents, too, did not know. And that thought was far worse than just her not knowing, so she sat silently wondering why her father seemed so calm when he, too, had left everything behind. The plane suddenly seemed very loud, its engines creating an ungodly din. Her seat was vibrating, the plane's musty smell was overpowering, and it was making her queasy. *This is not what flying is really like*, she told herself, *this is a military airplane.* She closed her eyes and tried to picture herself in a luxurious seat in a pleasantly scented cabin, the plane floating nearly silently as if carried gently along by a cloud. A jolt of turbulence snapped her from that reverie. She closed her eyes again and tried to picture herself in a pleasant apartment, beautifully decorated. She imagined wearing some American clothes—vivid colors and scratchy, cheap fabric. Her vision was interrupted by an announcement from the pilot telling the refugees that they would be landing in America in about half an hour.

✳ ✳ ✳

"Camp Kilmer" sounded so bizarre when Erzsi tried to say it out loud. She pronounced it "Cump Kill-mare." The name of the town it was in was even stranger—Piscataway—which her Hungarian instincts told her to say as "Pishcutuwuyee." Her father found out from one of the other refugees that this had been a very busy and active camp during the war but had only recently been reactivated to handle the Hungarian refugees that were coming to America by the thousands. And that was no exaggeration, the place was teeming with Hungarians.

It was both exhilarating and depressing to see so many of her people in this place called New Jersey. The sleeping quarters were army barracks, a place where the soldiers used to sleep. Uncle Ernő was supposed to arrive the next day to come get them, and Erzsi could not wait. Her eyes burned from being awake so long; her stomach was still queasy, and she felt grimy.

"I am told there are over one thousand buildings in this place," Mr. Molnár said as they were getting ready for bed. Around them, many other families were also settling in for the night. Erzsi watched a mother at the far end of the room trying to calm a toddler who wouldn't stop crying.

"It's a little bit overwhelming," said Mrs. Molnár.

"Can we say the prayer tonight?" Erzsi asked.

"I've wanted to say it with you every night, but you started protesting and saying it was for little children!" Mrs. Molnár said with a smirk. "But of course, we can say it."

"My God, good God, my eyes are already closing. But yours are open, Father. While I sleep, watch over me! Watch over my dear parents, and my brothers and sisters. When the sun rises again, let's kiss each other in the morning."

As she used to in the old days, Erzsi repeated each line after her mother said it. Mrs. Molnár kissed her forehead and told her to try to get some sleep, because tomorrow would be a big day. But truthfully, every one of the last thirty days or so felt like a big day.

"Happy New Year!" Lili whispered to her sister, who only then remembered that it was December 31 and tomorrow would be a brand-new year. The year 1957 would wipe 1956 off the calendar, and it could not be a more fitting start.

CHAPTER 30
January 1, 1957

Uncle Ernő was not what Erzsi had expected; he was almost nothing like his brother. He was four years younger and though he, too, was balding, he seemed decades younger than Mr. Molnár, if only in his demeanor. He offered his family New Year's greetings in Hungarian and English, with a big smile and warm hugs for everyone starting with Erzsi.

"Hello there, young lady. You must be Erzsébet."

"You may call me Erzsi." She bowed to him with a giggle.

He bowed back to her. "Very well then, Erzsi. I have heard much about you, and now I am honored to finally meet you. I hope you survived the plane ride okay." She was surprised that his Hungarian was intact after this long in America. She wondered whether she would ever forget how to speak her native language.

"We will see. There are moments when I feel like I am still on the plane," said Erzsi, and her uncle smiled and kissed her head.

Ernő moved on to her sister. "Lili, my dear Lili!" he said, beaming. "Look at that blond hair! You were just a year old when I last saw you. And look at you now. Clearly much older than that but still as blond as a field of wheat." He laughed. The family still knew him as Ernő Molnár, but here in America, he'd changed his name to something easier to pronounce: Ernie Miller. The new first and last names meant the same thing as the old ones, for what that was worth. Ernie was also the name of his favorite comedian, a Hungarian-American man named Ernie Kovacs.

"Well, obviously, I have no memory of that," Lili said sharply, but with a wry smile.

"You're an old lady now. It was quite long ago, so I barely have a memory of that either!" he said with a wink that caused Lili to giggle. This Ernő was a charmer to be sure.

"Anna! Darling! You've not aged at all and you're more radiant than ever before. It's so good to see you again," he said to his sister-in-law.

"You too, Ernő," she said, and Erzsi saw tears in her mother's eyes as they embraced. A familiar face from the past in an unfamiliar land was quite a relief, Erzsi imagined.

And finally, Ernő greeted his brother after seventeen years apart. "Well, Jancsi. It's been far too long!" He put his hand out and they shook, and then embraced a little bit awkwardly.

"You were so close to Hungary back in '45. It's too bad you could not have visited then," Jancsi said with a trace of sadness in his voice. His brother had served in the US army and was part of the Third Army's liberating force in central and eastern Europe. "How's the bead business treating you?"

"Oh, it's been good. Americans love costume jewelry. In fact, last year I sent twelve colorful strings of glass beads to Mrs. Eisenhower—you know, the president's wife."

All four of the Molnárs gasped. Uncle Ernő had a personal connection to the president! That was impressive. Mr. Molnár nodded slowly. "Well, then it's no wonder they let us in," he said quietly. Jancsi knew that to succeed in America, he would have start his own business, like his brother. And to get there, he'd have to work his way up, take whatever jobs came his way, and accept loans from Ernő, at least for a while, until the family got on their feet.

"I have no way of knowing if she is wearing them. Maybe she threw them straight into the trash. But in any event, she did send a letter thanking me for them. I will have to show you one day. There are many things I will have to show you. And, of course, the bead factory. I can always find a job for you there until you get settled," Ernő said.

"We, too, have a letter, but it's from the president himself," said Mr. Molnár. Erzsi knew that the thought of working for his little brother was abhorrent to her father. But she also knew he'd force himself to do it if it meant supporting his family.

"We do?" asked Erzsi, wide-eyed.

"Yes, you can read that later. They handed it to me when we arrived at Camp Kilmer."

"Ahh, but is your letter hand signed?" Ernő asked.

"Maybe it is, we'll see," said Mr. Molnár, and Erzsi could hear a touch of brotherly competition in his voice. "For now, let's get out of here. Where's your car, Ernő?"

He led them to the parking lot and his Buick, a hulking, solid sky-blue car with four doors that was unlike anything Erzsi had ever seen in Budapest, where the vehicles were smaller and, in Erzsi's opinion, less attractive. They put their few possessions into the spacious trunk and the three girls sat in the back while Mr. Molnár sat in the front with his brother. The engine roared to life but to Erzsi the sound was so soothing—not a train or plane, it was just a car taking them to their new home. To a bed. And a bath.

They drove on some local roads first and then the Buick merged onto a busy highway. Cars of all sizes and colors whizzed by, and big trucks barreled along. One honked its obnoxious horn at Ernő, startling Erzsi so much she hit her head on the roof of the car.

"Welcome to life on the interstate. The I-95, as they call it," Ernő said.

"A far cry from Andrássy Street," Mrs. Molnár said. The family hadn't owned a car, so their experience on Hungary's roads outside Budapest was quite limited.

"Speak some English, Uncle," Erzsi said. "Let's see how it sounds from the mouth of a Hungarian. I want to know what I'm going to sound like in a year or two."

"*Sure, I can speak some English for you, though I don't think you'll understand a single word of it. But one day it'll come very naturally to you, just give it time.*" And he was right, she understood nothing, though from his tone it sounded as if he were trying to impart some reassuring thoughts. He sounded magnificent and alien; he spoke so quickly and fluently.

"All right, enough showing off, Ernő. You've been here seventeen years. I'd expect you to be able to speak the language."

"Tsk tsk. He wasn't showing off, Erzsi asked him to talk in English," Mrs. Molnár said. And with that, silence descended on the passengers for the next several minutes. The ride was a little dizzying. Ernő was going very fast and the pavement was rough at times. But it was not nearly as unsettling as the airplane had been. Being on the ground was great, no matter how bumpy it was. Erzsi was a little squished sitting in between her mother and sister, but she didn't mind the contact, it was comforting.

After a while on the interstate, they went into a long tunnel. "This is the Lincoln Tunnel, named after one of the most famous presidents, Abraham Lincoln."

"Hmm. Did you send his wife beads too?" Lili asked, laughing.

"I would have if I could, trust me," said Ernő.

When they emerged from the tunnel, they were in New York—the world's most populous city—a fact that Ernő proudly announced as if he were that overenthusiastic tour guide they'd had a couple of years back on the boat tour of Lake Balaton.

The streets were bumpy and there were taxis everywhere, and cars, and motorcycles, and buses, and pedestrians crisscrossing the street, and bicyclists weaving in and out of the traffic. Ernő told them to roll down their windows to better see everything; when they did, the exhaust from the bus in front of them made Erzsi cough.

The buildings were so tall, reaching far higher than anything she'd known in Hungary.

"But this is not the best part of the city right here. We're on the west side of Manhattan, but wait until we get closer to Midtown; then the views will be better," he said, swerving to avoid a motorcycle that had cut in front of him.

"Eh, this is no worse than Budapest on an average day," scoffed Mr. Molnár. Erzsi knew he was trying to be brave and that this actually terrified him.

"Hmm, I guess Budapest is worse than I remember it . . ."

"Oh, be quiet." And they both laughed.

It was kind of fun to see that Mr. Molnár had his match in Ernő. The car stopped at a red light, next to a sign that said Fifth Avenue. Ernő told them to look to the left and that all the great things in the city were that way—Rockefeller Center, Radio City Music Hall, St. Patrick's Cathedral, and Central Park, to name a few. When the light changed and they proceeded across Fifth, Erzsi craned her neck to see any of those places, but it was just an avenue with fancy shops housed in old buildings—impressive but not as nice as Sztálin Street. And if there was a park it was nowhere in sight.

"Where are we going?" she finally asked. She was immediately shushed by her mother, but Uncle Ernő answered. He seemed like quite a patient man, perhaps because he had no children.

"We are going to Queens," he said, and he translated it into Hungarian. Queens! How elegant.

"Well, isn't that fancy," said Lili, who had been quiet for the last half hour.

"Yes, it is rather fancy. And there is also a place next to Queens County called Brooklyn, also known as Kings County. That is where my bead factory is!"

"So we will be neighbors then!" Erzsi said with a clap of her hands. She was becoming fonder of Uncle Ernő by the minute. He seemed intelligent and also just very accepting of this branch of his family he'd not seen in so long.

"You can say that, yes."

"What are we going to do about furniture? We have nothing." Lili brushed the windblown hair out of her eyes.

"This apartment is furnished. It comes with tables and chairs and beds and the like. Nothing crazy, just the basics. You'll find it acceptable, I'm sure. Given the circumstances."

What a concept! So it won't be as depressing as walking into an empty place. More like a hotel. She dared not ask how long they would be staying at the apartment, and was soon distracted by the bridge they were crossing from Manhattan to Queens. There was traffic, though, and they crawled across the bridge. The cozy feeling of being between her mother and sister was now stifling. She felt trapped, pressed between their two coats, in a sea of cars inching across this steel bridge on the way to their new home.

✳ ✳ ✳

When they finally made it over the bridge, everyone was asking Ernő where the apartment was. Is this it? Is that it? He laughed. "Ahh, but Queens is huge. There are many neighborhoods, and this apartment happens to be in one called Woodside. It's about fifteen more minutes, I think, maybe less if the traffic is good and we hit all the lights."

Queens was very different from Manhattan. There was really nothing to ooh and aah about. The buildings were not very tall and the boulevard they were on—Queens Boulevard—was wide but inelegant (very!); there were no trees, and it was lined not with regal apartment buildings or cafés but with auto repair shops and motels and modern-looking restaurants with colorful signs. Ernő explained again that they were still in New York City, even though it did not look like it one bit. He tried to use an example from Budapest to explain this to them.

"Think of Újpest, it's very different from the heart of downtown."

"It's different all right, but this is . . . more than different," Lili said.

"You'll get used to it soon enough. There are a great many Hungarians in Queens. Thousands. One of my old high school teachers is in Forest Hills, Dr. Lajos Nemzeti. You missed him by one year, Jancsi, he came in just after you graduated. Anyway, he lives in a great big apartment building on Queens Boulevard with his two mischievous Persian cats and is happy as can be. Me and Aunt Maria had dinner there a few months back. There are also some good Hungarian bakeries and shops around. You'll find them all eventually, you'll connect with others, and you'll feel quite at home here. I could give you some names and addresses but it's probably better that you explore and find them on your own. In Manhattan there's also a section called Little Hungary that has a high concentration of our people. And a Hungarian Catholic church—yes, I forgot to mention that. St. Stephen Church on Eighty-Second Street." Ernő was gesturing wildly with his right hand while his left steered the car along the boulevard, and Erzsi was reminded of a salesman making a pitch. It was cute how excited he was to show his family New York, but she was skeptical of the Hungarian flavor he was so keen on stressing. So far, she'd not seen a single Hungarian name on any shop or restaurant sign. They were all very generic names like Johnson and Andrews and Daniels. As if reading her mind, Ernő added: "Don't bother looking for Hungarian presence here, the main Hungarian areas are Rego Park and Forest Hills, further east down the boulevard. This is not really a residential neighborhood here anyway, it's more industrial. The Hungarian shops are located where the Hungarians live."

Mr. Molnár was normally a rather argumentative and inquisitive person, but Ernő's superior knowledge presented in a rapid-fire information overload, combined with the exhaustion of the last twenty-four hours, had clearly worn him down. Erzsi had seen it in his face when they were being picked up at Camp Kilmer. In fact, though they were all listening to Uncle Ernő, Erzsi figured that none of them would remember a word he said, and they'd have to ask him everything again after they'd all had a decent night of sleep.

Ernő finally turned off Queens Boulevard (praise the Lord!) and down a side street, handing his brother a piece of paper to navigate the directions as he drove. Left here, right at the light, another right a few blocks later, then an immediate left. And then Mr. Molnár read out an address, which was not a simple number but was two numbers with a dash between them. And the street itself was also numbered. Ernő found a parking spot and they got out. Erzsi's legs were sore from being cramped. She stretched and then looked at her surroundings. They were on a pleasant enough street, but all the buildings looked exactly the same—plain-looking modern two-story brick buildings each with two adjacent doors. Ernő asked for the paper and checked the address against the building they were standing in front of.

"I thought you said you personally checked this place out," Mr. Molnár said, shaking his head. "You don't seem to have any clue where you are. It's a little like the old days, isn't it?" Ahh, there was the feisty Mr. Molnár she knew and loved.

"Oh, I did, I was here last week. But as you see, the houses are very similar to each other. Just want to be sure I've got the right place. And I do. This is it. Yes, the broken flower pot on the side of the steps, I remember that distinctly!"

"Broken flower pot," Lili said. "Welcome to America."

"Not a bad size, I guess," Mrs. Molnár said, studying the

building, peering up at the second floor then down again at the first.

Ernő held up a hand. "Now, well, keep in mind that this is not one apartment—it's four. Two on each side, upstairs and downstairs. You'll be in the one on the left, upstairs. And this is only for now, until we figure out something more permanent."

He took a key ring out of his pocket and jingled the two brass keys. "The landlord knows you're moving in either today or tomorrow, so we can just go right in. You're all paid up for the week. I've got a couple of other places for us to look at in the next few days, but this was just to get you a place that was more comfortable than a hotel."

"For the week?" Mrs. Molnár asked, confused. "Is this a hotel?"

"Yes, this apartment is a weekly rental. Because there are people who need that. Like you. As I said, just until we find something better that you pick for yourself. I certainly didn't want to lock you into a place for a year, which you didn't see and approve of first. Most apartments have a one-year lease. This one is just a weekly rental, so it's just what you need for now."

He unlocked the red metal front door, which squeaked loudly, and the Molnárs followed Ernő inside, up a flight of bare wooden stairs, and to a flimsy wooden door on the left, for which he used a different key. Inside, it smelled of mothballs and furniture polish, and it was dark because all the blinds were pulled. Ernő quickly let the light in and threw open the two windows by the entrance, facing the street where they'd parked. There was a living room that connected directly to a bright but cramped kitchen, two small bedrooms that together were maybe as large as the sisters' bedroom back in Hungary, and a tiny bathroom with a yellow tile floor, a toilet with what looked like a piece of thick brown carpeting on the top of the seat, and a shower stall but no bathtub. The wood furniture was minimal, and what was there was old and scuffed. Yet to Erzsi it looked like paradise. It was strange and alien but still it felt like home.

CHAPTER 31
January 1

No sooner had they walked around their new apartment than two boys in matching red and white striped shirts burst into their living room. One was a couple of years younger than Erzsi and the other a couple of years older.

"*New neighbors!*" the younger one blurted breathlessly in English.

"*Hello boys, nice to see you again,*" Ernő replied to them. "*Your new neighbors are very lovely people, but I'm afraid they don't speak much English at all.*"

The older boy and Ernő had a brief conversation and then Ernő turned to Erzsi and said in Hungarian: "So the boys would like to invite you to watch a little television with them, in their apartment. There are cartoons on now. I told them you are probably tired and overwhelmed, but that I'd ask you."

Erzsi smiled broadly and said one of the few words she knew in English: "Yes!"

The boys clapped their hands and she followed them to the downstairs apartment, which was laid out exactly the same as theirs, only with much more furniture so it actually seemed smaller. In their living room was a big television set. The boys gestured for her to join them on the couch. Their mother introduced herself, but Erzsi did not understand the name she said. It sounded like "Mrs. L and Or Englehoffer," but she did not want to ask the nice woman to repeat herself. She said her own name and then turned toward the television set. Mickey Mouse was on the screen, and Erzsi watched in wonder at the antics of this cartoon character, the likes of which she'd never seen. For a few minutes at least, she forgot everything else that had happened. She even forgot there were strange boys sitting next to her. It was a good feeling.

* * *

A couple of hours later, when Erzsi sat down on the edge of her new bed for the first time, the springs creaked loudly. She could feel the hard metal coils under her. She was still in shock at what her father had told her a few minutes before—that tomorrow she would be going to school. She protested that it was too soon. School! An American school! She should have been back in her school in Budapest, where she belonged. She wondered whether Margit was still in Hungary, or whether she had escaped too. Would her classmates or teacher even miss her? She was in no mood to go to school here in New York. Before Mr. Molnár could reply, Uncle Ernő gently said that it was best for her to start her American education as soon as possible, so she could understand what

Mickey Mouse was actually saying. She laughed nervously and said okay.

"Wanna switch beds?" she asked her sister, who ignored her and climbed onto her own bed clutching one of the American magazines Uncle Ernő had given her. She propped herself up with the two pillows and leafed through the pages.

"Can I have one of those to read?" she asked.

"First of all, it's in English so you won't be able to read a thing. Second, this is boring stuff, you won't enjoy it," Lili said. "It's about gardening. Not that I am thrilled either, but I need something mindless right now, and there are a lot of pictures of flowers and trees to look at."

Erzsi reached over to the nightstand and unfolded the letter from President Eisenhower that her father had let her borrow. So many words, she could only imagine what it said.

She could hear her parents talking to Ernő in the living room. It was comforting having him there. She actually dreaded him leaving them all alone in America, in New York City. She was looking forward to tomorrow evening; they were invited to dinner with Uncle Ernő and Aunt Maria, after they settled in and got some rest. And as if on cue, Ernő walked into the bedroom and said it was time for him to go, that their aunt was waiting for him.

She studied his kind face, his wise brown eyes behind the round spectacles, his balding head.

"What's that you have?" he asked his niece.

"The magazines you gave me," Lili said.

"No, I mean you, Erzsi." He smiled gently. Erzsi knew she would love this man very much; she already did. He was a gentler and subtler version of her father.

"It's the letter from the president. I can't understand it though."

He nodded and held out a hand. "If you would like I can read it to you before I go."

By now, Mrs. Molnár and Mr. Molnár had come into the bedroom as well. "Yes, do read it," Mrs. Molnár said before her husband could object. She knew he was tired and wanted to get to bed soon, but Erzsi could see her mother was curious about the letter too.

Ernő read the letter in English, translating one sentence at a time into Hungarian as he went along. His English was perfect, at least to Erzsi's unfamiliar ears.

My friends from Hungary,

On behalf of my fellow Americans, I welcome you to the United States.

The circumstances that have separated you from your homeland and your loved ones fill American hearts with deep emotion and with compassion for what you are enduring. We feel a solemn and responsible pride that in your time of need you have come to our shores.

Through the centuries, the Hungarian people have bravely resisted oppression. Their courageous spirit continues today to inspire free people everywhere.

It has been our American heritage to assert our individual freedom and to offer to other peoples, struggling for their own liberty as we once did, such assistance and asylum as we can.

At first our land and our laws may seem very strange to you. Some necessary processes through which you join our way of living may cause you minor inconvenience but I ask you to think always of what, beneath these forms, dwells in our American hearts—an earnest desire to clasp your hands, to reach mutual understanding, and to become firm friends and neighbors.

Thus, we welcome you to American soil. We realize that you ardently hope for a time when all Hungarians can enjoy the blessings of individual freedom in their Hungarian mother-country. We join in that hope. And we give you this present assurance—if, when that day dawns once more, you should choose to go back to your native homes in Hungary, America will do its best in helping you to return.

Dwight D. Eisenhower

✳ ✳ ✳

She was exhausted, but her eyes did not want to close, because if they did then the day would be over and the next day would be coming and it would be the first full day of the rest of her life, here in America. She didn't want today to end, this in-transit, feet-in-both-worlds, old Erzsi–new Erzsi day. Even at Camp Kilmer, she had still felt a connection to her old life, a connection to the refugee center in Vienna. But this was real now, this was an apartment in

New York. She was scared that when she woke up it would be gone, all of it. She would wake up an American.

She lay there on her back, staring at the ceiling. The blinds were drawn but light from the driveway next door still filtered in. Lili was asleep and her parents were probably asleep too. Lili had left the stack of gardening magazines on the floor between their beds. Erzsi leaned down and took the top one. Maybe pictures of flowers would help her sleep. The magazine had a scent, not of flowers but of old paper, of must. The issue in her hands was from July 1953. Three years, but it seemed like forever ago. She struggled to remember what life was like back then when she was seven. It was just a happy blur of faces and places. She opened the magazine and turned the pages slowly, nervous to wake her sister and be yelled at. There was more text than she'd hoped, but interspersed were four-page spreads of just photos. She studied them in the dim light. Toward the middle of the magazine was an article titled "The Eisenhowers and the White House Gardens," and it featured big, beautiful color pictures of red roses and other pink and purple flowers she could not identify. On the third page of the article was a photo of the president and the first lady standing in the garden. He had a long-stemmed red rose in his hand and was presenting it to his wife. He looked kindly and thoughtful, like a man who would have written that letter to them. His face actually reminded her a lot of Uncle Ernő's. The same kindness and concern, the same bald head. She put the magazine back on the pile, turned on her side, and pulled the blankets up to her neck.

"I welcome you to the United States," she repeated softly and smiled, then gently closed her eyes, the president's letter safely tucked under her pillow right alongside the folded sketch of the October 23 rally. As she drifted off to sleep, she imagined herself as Marta, painting a bright red rose on a fresh white canvas.

The End